D0926259

Claimed by Fate

NEW YORK TIMES BESTSELLING AUTHOR

SHANNON
MAYER

To that one person who thought
I should write newspaper articles,
because writing books would never
be anything more than a hobby at best...
thanks for the motivation to keep going,
if for nothing else than to prove you wrong.

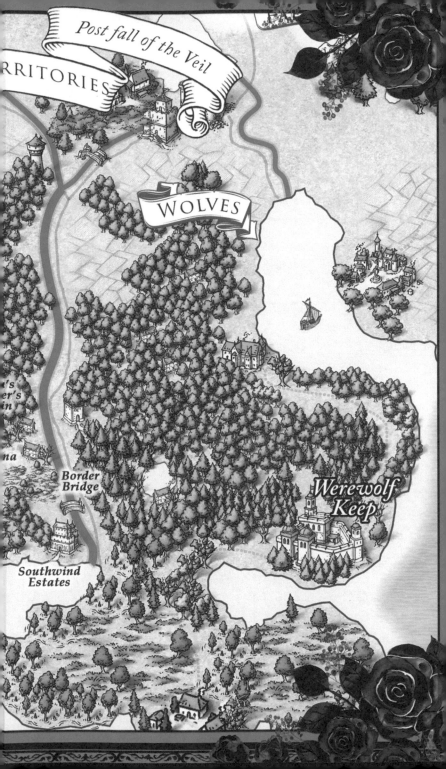

CHAPTER 1

Sienna

Grief flowed in and out of me, like the edge of the ocean that pulled at the sand of the beach, drawing my feet forward with each brush of the icy water against my ankles. There were no tears, though my heart had cracked in half.

There had been no time for anything. The last two days had been a blur. Dominic had a plan, one that should have been foolproof. The plan? His captain of the guard, Scarlett, had secretly arranged for the Vanators to take out Edmund the Vile.

Scarlett was to have brought Edmund out to the North Fort, where the Vanators—human vampire hunters—would ambush him, take his head and end his reign. William, Dominic's younger brother, would then sweep in and 'drive out' the Vanators, and take his place as king of the Vampire Territory.

Nothing had gone right.

Scarlett had turned on Dominic.

Edmund had killed the one insider Dominic had in Frank Eleazar.

The Vanators had been scattered, and worst of all...Jordan had been killed.

My Jordan.

The boy I'd come to rescue, the boy who was like a brother to me, had been shot down by Scarlett herself.

Eyes closed, I could see Jordan clearly as he took his last breath in my arms, the light from his eyes gone so quickly there was no chance of healing him.

Goodbye, CeeCee.

I swallowed hard and drew in a slow breath, unable to cry. There were so many fractures in my heart that if I started, there would be no stopping the flood. The funeral would begin shortly, but I needed...something. Maybe just a moment to think. The fog of pain was wrapped so tightly around me, I just knew that I couldn't face anyone else. Not yet.

A thin, light blue tentacle slid out of the water, the tip of it touching my bare calf.

The kraken's own grief added to mine, but still the dam of tears didn't break, the pressure building in my chest until it felt like I was wrapped in metal bands, tightening with each breath.

I had come all this way for Jordan, fought to get to him, schemed my way to get close, only to have him ripped away.

Would he ever have agreed to come with you?

Did you even truly want to leave?

My own thoughts were traitorous, driving wedges between what was true and what I wanted to be true. The fantasy of saving Jordan and us going home to the mainland. Home to a place where at least I fully understood the dangers and could navigate them.

But would he have been happy? He died here, a hero. With a family that loved him.

A horn blew softly behind me, a mournful bugle call signaling the beginning of the funeral and cutting off my thoughts.

I bent and touched the kraken's tentacle briefly before heading back up the beach. In a numb haze, I dusted off my feet and tugged my socks and boots on.

Lochlin was about thirty feet away from me, giving me space, but also shadowing me. After the attacks on me—two now, in case anyone was counting—Diana was not taking any chances. I refused to think that Dominic had anything to do with me being watched over.

He'd been leading the army that Jordan had joined. He should've known. He should have done... something.

Rational? Nope, not one bit. But grief knew no sense when it filled every cell of your body and mind.

The clouds above us dusted the sky, hiding the stars and the swelling moon. Not full yet, but we were close. I turned my face to the heavens, wishing for rain, and thunder, and lightning. Wishing for the weather to reflect my pain.

I made my way to where the funeral was set to take place. The burial mounds were set to the north of the keep, the entrance of it planted with a tree I didn't know, and that I had to step through. The trees most similarly matched a weeping willow, only the trunks, leaves, and branches were inky black. Dark, and yet shimmering with iridescence across every part, even by the dim light of the stars. The trees looked as if they had burned to a crisp and then somehow still lived on and grew. I watched them move and sway gently in the wind.

Only there was no wind.

I lifted a hand to part the black leaf curtain and gasped.

The trees were moving on their own. The whip-slim branches slid over me, the leaves brushing across my face like velvet fingers, stroking my cheeks. If I'd been crying, they would have brushed the tears away.

This place could be so cruel—so terrible at times, and then something magical...miraculous, even, would happen, making my head spin.

I moved past the trees, reluctantly leaving their embrace, and stared at the scene that spilled out in front of me. The black willows had given way to a massive clearing that had to be two football fields in size, and yet only a small section of it was taken up.

The wolf packs were gathered around a single body laid out on a waist-high platform.

I moved on autopilot straight for Jordan. He was gone, his body just a shell now. I knew it in every part of my heart and soul and yet there was this stupid hope that he was playing. That he would sit up and tell me it was a joke, that he wasn't really gone.

I reached his side and looked down at his face. He looked so peaceful; he could have been sleeping. A soft smile touched his lips, and his eyes were shut tight. His hands had been set on his chest, holding a sword.

Was it the one he'd carried into battle with him? The battle he never should have been in. A battle he'd joined in secret so he could prove to his new family that he was worthy of becoming one of them.

My jaw trembled as the emotions swelled along with memories that cut me through and through.

Finding Jordan on the street, nearly frozen to death when he'd been barely eight. How brilliant he'd been, surviving on his own for years. Smarter than me by far, and yet he'd looked to me for protection. The accident that had stolen so much from him, the head injury that should have never happened. Nursing him through that, knowing that he was the only family I had through the last five years.

I touched the spot where the arrow had pierced his heart. How he'd survived long enough to get back to the keep, to say his goodbye was beyond me. Maybe it was some twist of fate to push me in the direction that I needed to go.

Or needed to stay, as the case was.

I tugged the bracelet off my wrist, not even counting how many beads were left. I'd threaded them to track the days until we were supposed to meet our ship and make our escape. But that didn't matter.

Not anymore.

"I'm so sorry I couldn't save you," I whispered, bending over his upper body and pressing my lips to his forehead. "Little brother, I will find a way to make her pay. I swear it on my life."

With great care, I slipped the bracelet onto his wrist and then laid his hand back gently.

A woman I didn't know stepped forward. Her dark chestnut hair was streaked with gray on one side, her deep brown eyes were on me. She said nothing as she stepped closer to Jordan, across from me.

"My boy..." Her voice caught on those two words, and she fell forward onto Jordan's upper body, holding him. One last time.

I swallowed a moan before it could slide out of me and stepped back. One by one, his new family stepped up to say their goodbyes.

Each of them shed tears without any shame that I could see.

Each of them made sure to put their nose to Jordan's. A goodbye that shouldn't have been for any of them.

I stepped back further and further, until I was nearly to the black willows again. The werewolves ranged around the platform that Jordan lay on, torches lit, flicking and casting light over the night.

A large bear of a man stepped up, his grizzled face giving away his age if the white in his dark hair had not.

"This night, the clan Killian bids adieu to our boy, Jordan. Pure of heart, gentle of hand, he loved his family." His eyes slid over to me. "All of his family, wherever they be, he loved them with all his mighty heart."

My lower lip trembled, and my body shook, but I held it together. Barely.

"He went to prove himself a warrior, a fighter, for the glory of clan Killian. Not because he was asked to, but because he wanted to become one of us. I can only hope that he knew, in our hearts, he already was."

The woman with the white streak through her hair let out a sob that rippled the air.

I bit my lower lip and found myself staring across the circle at Dominic. His eyes were locked on me, and, for a moment I could see my pain reflected in them before I looked away. Bee was standing not far from Will, her head bowed, and her arms wrapped around her middle. She barely knew Jordan, but I had no doubt she'd grieve on my behalf. That was the kind of friend she was.

The best kind.

"And this night, we bid Jordan a safe journey from this world into the next, lifted up by our voices, held safe always, in our hearts." The alpha of clan Killian took the closest torch, turned it upside down and snuffed it on the ground.

One by one, like a rippling wave from his left, the torches were put out all around the circle until the clearing was a dark and shadowy place.

Silence, absolute silence.

Until a single voice broke it, a low mournful howl that was barely there, then grew in volume and strength. Joined by another wolf's howl, then another and another. It was not a cacophony, but a blending and harmonizing of voices that spoke to me even though I didn't understand it.

Grief, pain, love, hope. A goodbye that Jordan deserved, one that he never would have had if he'd died on the mainland. There we'd be lucky for a shallow grave.

The song of the wolves cut through me, unlocking the last of the hold I had on my emotions.

They loved him. They loved him fiercely even though he'd been with them a short time. If I'd never come here, he'd never have gone to battle. He'd still be alive. The sob caught me unawares, the need to howl my own pain to the sky, to join in with the wolves was overpowering. I slapped my hand over my mouth as the sobs erupted out of me, tears spilling down my cheeks as the song of Jordan's family tore away the last shred of control I had.

Stumbling back, eyes wide as my tears fell, I backed right up to the edge of the black willows. The trees shivered and danced, the velvet soft petals sweeping away the moisture from my cheeks as fast as it appeared.

I went to one knee, feeling the howls to my bones, aching in my very soul. Jordan should never have died, but...he deserved this mourning and more from the ones who loved him. The song ended as softly as it had begun, trailing away to nothing, leaving the clearing in silence once more.

"Lass," Lochlin's voice was thick, and he crouched beside me but didn't touch me. "The Killian alpha and his mate would like to meet you proper."

A shiver of exhaustion rolled through me, but I nodded and pushed to my feet once more.

Lochlin motioned for me to follow him, and again I found myself staring across at Dominic. Diana and Will were still by his side, but Bethany was gone.

Dominic never looked away from me as I followed

Lochlin to the man who was Killian's pack alpha.

"You be Jordan's sister, CeeCee. I be Kavan." He thrust out a hand to grip my forearm.

I blinked and tried to find my voice, but it was scratchy and still full of tears. "Found family. We weren't biological—"

"Bah, blood is blood, but choosing your family, there be strength and true bonds in that too. Sometimes more. Jordan spoke of you often. Said you protected him. Said he expected you to show up any day to be with him." He chuckled. "'O' course, we never dissuaded him of that dream. Though we knew it be impossible." Kavan squinted at me. "But then again, I hear you do the impossible, so he knew more than we did."

I just nodded; I had no words. Jordan had *known* I would come. The thought only made the tears fall more.

Kavan brushed rough fingers over both of my cheeks. "No more tears, not for Jordan. He's safe now. No one can hurt him anymore. And we will have that murderess's blood for the pain she caused us all."

I blinked up and took hold of both his hands, feeling a powerful bond growing between myself and this man I'd only just met. I squeezed them as tight as I could. "I will kill her myself, if it is the last thing I do."

He growled his approval. "I believe you. Welcome to the clan, little one."

I tipped my head sideways as he pinned Jordan's clan badge, still covered in dried blood, to the front of my leather vest. Then he pulled me into a bear hug and handed me off to his mate who—smelling distinctly of whiskey—did the same.

"I be Maya, Jordan's mum. Welcome to the clan, CeeCee." She squeezed me tight, and I hugged her back, letting myself sob with her. I didn't know why they were making me a member of their clan, but I could not deny that it meant something to me. To have Jordan's found family accept me, too.

I was passed around to each member of the Killian clan until they'd all bear hugged—or maybe wolf hugged—me to the point of my ribs aching in time with my heart. I was offered drinks but turned them all down.

This was not the time, not for me.

I made my way back toward Jordan, but his body had been removed and laid in the ground while the clan had welcomed me.

His body was covered in a fine coating of dirt, I could

just see his hands through it.

The final image broke me, and I turned and ran from the clearing, through the black willows and toward the ocean once more.

"Sienna," Dominic's voice dragged me to a stop like no other could have.

I turned around to face him in silence.

"I'm...so sorry, Sienna. I didn't know he was there in the battle. If I had known, I would have made him stay behind. I would have gotten him out of there or found a way to keep him safe. I know what he meant to you." He held a hand to me, asking for my forgiveness. Asking for me to step toward him.

Did I believe him? Yes, I suppose I did. I knew Dominic would never have just let Jordan die. But it didn't change the fact that Jordan *was* dead. Nothing of what happened could be changed by a few words or an apology. It wasn't like he was saying he was sorry for hurting my feelings, or for eating the last tart. Dominic was the General, in charge of that army, and he missed it. He missed the fact that Jordan had joined them, and it had cost me my best friend. I just couldn't forgive that. Not today. I needed time.

In the end, there was nothing for me to say, so I did the

only thing I could do without shattering.

I turned and walked away.

CHAPTER 2

Dominic

Sienna walked away from me, toward the ocean, and I could sense the pain coming off her in waves.

"Fuck me," I growled under my breath, raking both hands through my hair. I'd rather she rage at me, tell me I was an asshole, scream to the heavens. But she wasn't doing any of those things.

I smelled Lochlin before he joined me to watch Sienna make her way along the ocean's edge, the kraken following in her wake, then turn toward the keep.

"Come on, she can't be that far away from me," he said.

My jaw ticked, possessiveness rolling hard through me. "She's not yours to protect."

"Aye, well, even if that were true before, it isn't anymore. Clan Killian just made her part of the family," Lochlin said without breaking stride.

I, on the other hand, felt my feet go leaden.

"Wait, what?"

"Jordan vouched for her before the battle, the clan had already voted to bring her in so he wouldn't feel like he had to choose. I vouched for her of course, and I knew that it would give her added protection from the attacks from within the community." Lochlin stared ahead, never looking at me. "This is where you say thank you."

By taking her into their clan, he was right, Sienna was far more protected. And it wasn't like any vampire household would take her on as an adoptive member. I knew this. Yet it still gutted me like a fish on a line to think of Sienna staying *here* once the war was over.

Lochlin paused in his steps, we'd drawn close enough to Sienna apparently. "Man, what is wrong with you?"

"I love her."

Lochlin grunted as if I'd sacked him. "Well...at least you can admit it out loud."

It was the first time I'd said it, but I'd known it for a while now. When I was near death, the sun's rays sizzling me to the point of no return as I tried to rescue her from the kraken, it had suddenly been so clear.

Yes, I wanted to fuck her.

Yes, I wanted to own her.

But it was more than that. I loved her with every part of

me. It was a sensation I was still getting used to, made all the more difficult by the fact that she could hardly look at me right now.

"We aren't going to keep her, Dom," Loch continued. "She can do as she pleases with her life, we aren't like you lot."

Relief flowed through me, which was so fucking stupid. If I'd been thinking, I would have realized that the rules around clans were very different than our own.

I nodded. "One other thing."

"Aye?"

"I'm...sorry for being an ass. Before."

"Which time?" Lochlin laughed and then waved me off. "Fine. I'll forgive you this time. Next time I'll stake you."

I laughed low and mirthless with him. "I might ask you to do that anyway. If we lose to Edmund, a quick death would be a mercy."

My friend grunted and we started again to follow Sienna as she moved into the keep.

"Diana wants to speak with you," Lochlin said at an intersection of hallways, "I'll keep an eye on Sienna."

I nodded and he smacked me on the back of the shoulder, sending me down the hall in the opposite direction, his laugh following me. The man was never mad for long. It was why our friendship had endured.

Diana's rooms were on the upper floor, and I climbed the stairs with my mind only partially on the funeral and Sienna. For now, she was safe, and there was nothing I could do to make her see that Jordan's death lay at the feet of one person and one person only.

Scarlett was the one to blame. And that's where my mind went and blurred into an anger born of confusion and shock.

I could not understand how my trusted captain, friend, and sometimes bedfellow had turned on me and sided with Edmund. How long had she been working with him? Was she in league with him this whole time?

When I'd seen her last at the hunting cabin in the woods with Edmund, she'd locked eyes with me for the briefest of moments...

Had that been it then? Or was it long before that? Did it even matter?

She'd betrayed me. Cost us the battle, the life of Sienna's best friend, and dragged us into a full-blown war, all to support my sadistic, power-mongering prick of a brother. She was as good as dead to me.

I reached the Queen's sitting room and snapped my knuckles against the thick wooden door.

"Enter," Diana called out.

I stepped through to find Evangeline there, sitting in a plush straight-backed chair, a glass of wine in her hand.

"It has been a long day, Nicky. Come, have a drink."

Diana shot a grin over her shoulder at me. "Nicky? Oh, that will stick, I think."

I grimaced and made my way to the center table and poured myself a glass of wine from the crystal decanter. The scent of blood was shallow, but I appreciated what would be a boost. I took a sip and nodded.

"My thanks, Di."

Diana laughed low and soft. "I thought perhaps you and Will would like to know all of it. The rest of the story of how I came to be here. There are many secrets in our family, and I find myself no longer wanting to carry the burden of them."

My eyebrows raised and I gave a nod. "I'll admit it is something else to realize you have a sister who there is no rumor or written note of anywhere in the royal libraries."

There was a knock at the door and Will entered. He'd been at the funeral, though I hadn't thought it was a good idea. His skin tone had taken a turn for the worst these past two days, and he once again smelled of sickness. The bloodworm was clearly no longer dormant, and something needed to be done or it would kill him yet. Sienna had helped with her blood, but so far, it had been a temporary fix. We had to find a way to get it out of him.

Another impossible feat.

"Sister," Will tipped his head at Diana. She shot him a tired smile and motioned for him to sit next to Evangeline.

"To start, some of what I know, I know because of our aunt," Diana waved a hand toward Evangeline who dipped her head. "But I will tell the story as best I can, and she may intervene where necessary to fill in the gaps."

"There is more than you've already told us?" William asked, his voice hoarse. "Why tell us now?"

Diana picked up her own glass, the amber liquid and smell of oak barrels giving away its contents. "Because I wish to start fresh. We are going to war against a powerful enemy—our own brother. If I should fall, I want to know that you will stand by my adoptive family, William. I want to know that you will carry on as I would. That you will help and support General Whalen, as he is next in line for the pack throne."

Will's face was set. "I swear it, on the moon gods, to follow through."

She smiled. "I know, I see it in you now. I was afraid when you first arrived. I have been kept in the shadows for many years. While the vampires knew that I was next in line for the throne here, I was not brought out and pranced about. My father—Lycan—feared you might see something in me, Dominic. You were the only advocate that Stirling ever sent. And we knew that your powers of perception were excellent. I think if you had not been so distracted by Sienna and your worry for Will, you would have wondered when you met me."

Of course, now that I knew she was my sister I could see our similarities. The angle of her eyes, the shape of her nose, even the half smile she gave, so like that of Will's. The clues were there, but she was right. I had been distracted.

"My mother was one of the earliest Harvest Game girls, only back then it was called the Testing. Her name was Catina," Diana said. "She was a beauty by all standards, fit of form, dark hair, green eyes. Stirling was intrigued, but she pushed him away. She was...brilliant in her game playing. And in the end, it cost her the life she was fighting to keep."

Evangeline nodded and picked up the thread. "Edmund was just a boy himself when Catina realized she was pregnant. She kept the baby a secret from Stirling, not hard as he had a harem of women at the time, even if Catina was his favorite. She kept it from everyone until the end when it was too late to change it."

"Why would she have wanted to change it?" Sienna asked from the doorway.

Diana motioned for her to come all the way in. "Because back then, it was rare to survive pregnancy as a human, with a vampire father. My mother believed she would be different. That's what I always thought, at any rate." She shot a glance toward Evangeline, who shook her head.

"That wasn't the case at all. Catina had spoken with the Oracle, who told her that a daughter would be born of her loins, and that daughter would rise in power and strength and be the one to set the world a-right after it was ripped asunder. That even if she paid the ultimate price, it would be worth it. In the end."

I sucked in a breath. "That would put the knowledge of the Veil falling far before what is commonly known. But even so, why would Catina do this, knowing her daughter would be in the center of danger?"

"She had another child," Evangeline said. "A child she'd had to leave behind."

"My older sister would be dead and gone by then," Diana said softly, swirling her drink, "But my mother didn't know that it would be the case. She saw only a way to keep both her children as safe as she could, even if it cost her own life. She died giving birth to me. The connection to a child that carries vampire blood meant that her own blood would not coagulate. She bled out."

Silence fell around the room, and it was Sienna who broke it. "There is nothing more powerful than a mother's love."

"Well said," Evangeline whispered. "I took the child, Diana, under my wing and raised her as my own. She was mostly human, with a touch of vampire in her. Enough that she would have aged slowly and been a potential mate for a vampire lord."

Diana snorted and laughed. "That never would have happened. I was a handful even then."

"You were, but that is beyond the point," Evangeline smiled at Diana. "I had never produced a child on my own. Catina and I had a friendship that no one else understood." The Duchess paused and stared into her drink. "I was in a meeting with Stirling the day that Edmund nearly killed Diana."

Sienna gasped. "But he would have been a child himself!"

"Exactly," Diana dipped her head in Sienna's direction. "He was not yet thirteen. Yet he understood that Diana could potentially be a threat to his throne. You see he'd heard the whisper of the Oracle, that Catina would give birth to a powerful girl child that would change the world. I suspect he thought this meant she would take the throne from him."

"Means I'm going to cut his fucking head off now," Diana growled.

I cut her a sharp look and a nod. "Now I can clearly see the resemblance between us."

She flashed her teeth at me in a mock smile. I recognized that look too.

Evangeline went on as if we had not interrupted her. "He took Diana with him to the ocean's edge on the pretense of playing. I had a maid always with Diana and she alerted me where they had gone. Because Edmund told the maid she could not follow, and she knew that was not acceptable. As quickly as I could, I took after him and found him holding Diana under the water."

A pin could have dropped and would have sounded like a gun going off.

"He was always a cruel child, full of avarice," Evangeline said. "But I hoped he would change as he aged. The only thing that happened is that he got better at hiding his acts, better at keeping his malevolence from any who could correct him."

Diana took a breath. "Evangeline brought me to Lycan to raise as his own, which he did. He also made me a werewolf."

Evangeline sniffed. "I would have spoken against it."

Lycan took that moment to enter the room. "But I did not give you the chance, I am aware, Eva."

Eva? Now that was interesting. I found myself pulled out of Diana's story long enough to look between the two oldest amongst us. The two who were resolutely not looking at one another.

"I survived the change," Diana said, "Though it was a close thing. I would not wish it on anyone. While many humans have become werewolves, it is a grueling process. More than that though, my vampire blood fought the change as if it were a living thing."

Lycan took the stage then. "I taught her to fight, taught her strategy and had her learn everything she could about the other territories. The Oracle regularly made visits until she stopped leaving her section of the forest, and she also taught Diana."

Diana motioned at me and Will. "When you two were born, I begged my father to offer you protection as he'd done for me. Of course, you were full blooded vampires, and even you, Dominic, though you were a bastard—"

"Correct," Sienna muttered under her breath, perhaps forgetting that we could all hear her clearly. Then again, maybe she knew exactly what she was saying.

"—you were far more protected than me. And perhaps you, Evangeline, knew better how to keep them safe?"

Evangeline put her wine glass on the table. "I made sure that Dominic was raised by his mother until he was of age to join the army. Even then there were attempts on his life. But he was strong and smart and survived them all."

I shook my head, "What?"

Lycan gave a low laugh. "Lad, please. The rockslide at Wing Falls? The bandits when you were fifteen? The first battle you were set at the head of? All were attempts of Edmund's to quietly bump you off. He knew that you were more likeable than himself. And until Will came along, you were the spare."

The spare.

Fuck. I'd never even thought it because I had no aspirations, because I was the bastard son.

"And by the time Will came along, you were a ready-made protector," Evangeline said. "You took that charge seriously."

I remembered that night well. "You told me that Edmund would kill Will given any chance and that I was to protect him at all costs. To be clear, I would have anyway."

Diana looked from me to Will. "I have seen that, a love between brothers that I didn't think was possible in the Vampire Territories."

There was a heavy moment. "Diana, I will protect you at all costs, I swear it. I will protect you as I protect Will. That is my job in this family, after all."

Diana blinked away what looked like a glimmer of tears. "Thank you. Now, if we are all satisfied with the terrible family we come from, shall we drink deep? Nicholas of Southwind is loyal to William, and has sent word that the Hunters are wreaking havoc as they travel north. Apparently, they are moving at their own pace, despite

Edmund's wishes, but there is no doubt Sienna was right. They're coming. It's only a matter of time."

I glanced at Sienna, who didn't react at all, and reached for my cup.

May the gods help us all.

CHAPTER 3

Sienna

"I would give my left pinky to be able to go back in time and refuse that first tankard of ale last night," Bee said with a groan, setting down the sword she'd been sharpening.

I nodded but didn't reply. Nothing good could come of it.

I wanted to tell her that, if we were trading body parts for time, I'd barter my very heart to go back and stop Jordan from sneaking away with the battalion headed to the North Fort. Instead, I held my tongue. She had joined the others, with the exception of Will and I, in drinking their woes away. It had worked...for a while. But they'd woken up this morning with the same worries they'd had the night before. And Bee, the only human in the bunch, had a brutal hangover to boot. Despite my grief that made me want to lash out at the world—deserved or not—I couldn't bring myself to add to her misery.

I thought back to the hurt in Dominic's eyes over the past couple of days, and my stomach clenched with guilt.

What was that saying? We always hurt the ones we—

"Sienna, come quickly, Lass!" Lochlin's booming voice carried into the courtyard where we sat, preparing weapons for the war to come.

Bee set down the sword and shot me a concerned look. "Hunters already?"

I shook my head grimly as I stood. "I don't think so. I'd have sensed them if they were close." No point in worrying her if I was wrong so I kept it to myself, but I had a pretty good idea why I was being summoned.

Together, we rushed toward the keep to find Loch standing in the doorway, clearly distraught.

"The young prince. He's taken a turn for the worse."

Bee let out an anguished gasp and clapped her hand over her mouth.

"Take us to him," I replied, my voice as calm as I could make it. I'd noticed Will's health declining and had offered him blood the night before, but he'd insisted he was fine, and I was too emotionally battered and bruised to argue. Now, as we rushed to Will's quarters, I hoped I didn't live to regret that decision.

When we walked into the room, Will was sitting up in his bed, surrounded by Dominic, Diana, Evangeline, and Lycan.

"What's happened? Are you alright?" Bee demanded, shouldering her way between the Queen and Duchess to kneel beside Will.

"I'm right as rain," he said, managing a weak smile.

"Acid rain, maybe," I replied, taking in his appearance. "You look like hammered shit...Your Grace," I added with a curtsy.

His smile grew wider just as I'd hoped. "I can always count on you to keep me humble, Sienna."

"This is true," I said, reaching up to pull the pin from my hair. "If only you would so easily count on me to keep you alive. I'm not asking this time, buddy. You're going to drink some blood and you're going to keep drinking until you feel better."

"It's not that simple, child," Evangeline murmured, her eyes suspiciously glassy in a way that made my heart give a squeeze. "We think..." she trailed off and glanced at Diana.

"We can't be certain," the Queen said, taking the reins, "But we believe that, while your blood helped force the bloodworm into a type of stasis at first, it's now become something of the opposite."

It had been a few days since Will last fed from me, but as she spoke, I realized she was right. He hadn't immediately improved like all the other times. In fact, in the days and even hours that followed, he'd seemed worse.

I frowned and shook my head. "But why?"

"I have a theory," Lycan interjected as he slipped a comforting arm around Evangeline's waist. "I think your blood was initially a shock to the creature's system. It had never tasted its kind."

"But now that the worm has adjusted, it seems like it's causing it to thrive," Will added, shifted in the bed with a wince. "I could feel it after the last time. I'd hoped maybe starving it would help, but it's only gotten worse. It's writhing...growing inside me now."

Bee's already pale, hungover face turned a sickly shade of green. "I can't—" she broke off and sucked in a shuddering breath. "So, what do we do? There has to be something."

The silence that fell over the room lasted far too long, and she shot to her feet.

"No. We can't just give up; I won't hear it. There has to be a way."

More silence as she wheeled toward me.

"You have all this magic. Can't you *do* something? You can talk to the Hunters and the kraken."

"They're sentient beings," I explained, not sure I even fully understood it myself. "When the Hunters were freed, I could sense fear from the birds and the deer in the woods nearby, but I don't have any connection with bugs or creatures like that."

Her cornflower eyes were wild with fear, and I wished I could say something to take it away, but I was at a complete loss.

"I suppose I could try to lay my hands on him as I did with Dom after he was burned, but..." I began slowly. Before I could finish, Diana was already shaking her head, completing my thought.

"But Will himself isn't technically sick. There is nothing to heal. If the worm thrives on your blood and you lay healing hands on Will, we risk making the worm even stronger."

"We need to get it out, then," Bee said, crossing her arms over her chest defiantly. "An operation, maybe? Has anyone even asked the surgeon if he can try?"

"That was one of the first things we did during the outbreak all those years ago," Dominic said with a frown.

"The worms have retractable hooks that sink into your bowels when you try to remove them forcibly. We can get the worm out, but Will's innards will come with it. As weak as he is, I fear he wouldn't survive that, vampire or not."

"Sienna can fix it," Bee shot back.

Diana shook her head slowly. "We've seen her powers help heal burned flesh, but to replace something that's completely gone? Is that even possible?"

"Maybe..." But even Bee sounded doubtful now.

"I'm not all that enthusiastic about the plan, but I fear if we don't come up with an alternative by nightfall, we might have to risk it." Again, he winced, his jaw tight with the pain. "I feel like it's taking over my whole body."

I could only imagine how much he was suffering and appreciated how hard he tried to hide it from us all.

From Bee.

She raked a hand through her hair and blew out a sigh. "Why can't you all have easier to kill parasites, like us humans? Take a pill, boom, it's gone most of the time. In fact, did you know, in the 1950's they used to sell tapeworms to housewives so they could keep their weight down?" she let out a semi-hysterical laugh that had me more worried than tears ever could. "They'd eat a bloody tapeworm to keep their tiny waists in check. How crazy is that?"

Will reached for her hand but she pulled away.

"Don't! Don't try to tell me it's going to be okay, because—"

She broke off suddenly and the color returned to her cheeks in a rush as her eyes popped wide.

"Bait," she breathed, wringing her hands together. "I remember reading something about how the women would get rid of their tapeworm back then. They would starve it and then bait it to come out on its own with warm milk."

"Seriously?" Will asked dubiously. "And that was a success?"

Bethany's cheeks went pink. "I don't remember."

"We've tried that," Evangaline said, shaking her head. "Long ago, many times. It didn't work."

"It didn't work with human or vampire blood," Bee pressed. "But what about with Sienna's blood. We all know it's magic. Surely, we can try?"

She sent a hopeful look toward Evangeline, who nodded and managed an encouraging smile.

"Alright. It's a good idea, Bethany. Let us try."

Bee turned to me then, a plea in her eyes. "Sienna?"

"Of course."

Twenty minutes later, we had the whole crazy thing set up. Loch, Bee, the Duchess, and Lycan stood close by, at the ready in case things didn't go to plan. I stood across the room with a blade in one hand and a towel in another. Will sat, chained to a chair at Dominic's insistence. Partly because Will was starving, and Dominic was afraid my blood would incite him. Partly because we needed Will to stay put no matter how much it hurt.

"I can imagine, if this thing exits as we hope, it's not going to be pleasant. We'll have the best chance of success if you remain as still as possible," Dominic explained grimly.

Will nodded, white knuckling the arms of his seat. "I'll do my best."

Dominic bent close to him then and cupped the back of Will's head. "That's all I can ask of you, brother."

A tender moment passed between them that made me look away.

This had to work. Losing Jordan had been terrible, destroying so much hope in me. If we lost Will now, it would mean Jordan's death was for nothing.

I refused to even think of what it would do to Dominic.

"Let's get it done," I said, using the blade to slice the back side of my wrist before moving to stand in front of Will. For a second, I locked eyes with Dominic, and I feared he was about to stop me. But I sidled past him, and he kept his hands clenched at his side.

I lifted my arm close to Will's face, heart pounding with fear. "Open your mouth," I instructed, watching as his pupils dilated and the fangs extended from his gums.

"Yesss," he hissed, nostrils flaring as he strained toward me.

"Will..." Dominic growled, stepping forward. The Duchess took hold of his forearm with a snick of her tongue.

"It's alright, Nicky. We're all here. She's safe."

Funny, but I didn't feel safe. I swallowed hard, focusing not on Will, but on the blood dripping down my fingers, just inches from Will's open mouth.

"Come on, you wormy bastard. Come on..." Bee whispered under her breath.

For a long moment, nothing at all happened, the silence broken only by Will's shallow breathing.

"Please," he begged, looking fevered now as he craned

his neck toward me in hopes of catching the crimson droplets on his tongue. But, suddenly, the yearning in his eyes turned to horror. He stiffened, his back bowing as he shook his head frantically. "No. No, move away—" his words were garbled as he broke off and began to wretch.

Dominic's calming hand on the small of my back was the only thing keeping me there as Will's neck began to swell, expanding like the gullet of a crane swallowing a catfish. In reverse.

My hand began to tremble, but I forced myself not to pull back even as Will's jaw widened and then cracked.

"Oh my gods...please," Bee whimpered, but I could barely hear her. I was too focused on the head of the creature creeping up Will's throat and out of his gaping maw.

Loch moved closer. "Hold steady, Lass. A few more inches and I think I can—"

The bloodworm launched itself out of Will's mouth like it had been shot out of a cannon, its razor-sharp teeth bypassing my bloody fingers and heading straight for my face.

I jerked to the side, covering my mouth with my hand even as Dominic shielded me with his body and knocked it to the ground.

The creature squealed, its three-foot long, tar-black form wriggling and writhing.

Sienna... You are fighting a war you cannot win. Go home.

The voice. So familiar...the same that I'd heard when I'd dreamt of daisies, death, and destruction. The same that had told me, if I stayed, I'd be the death of them all.

"Don't let it get away!" Lycan shouted.

But Loch was already on it, his broadsword ringing as he swung it high in the air. A second later, he lopped off its head with a sickening squelch. Its body continued to move for a few moments and then went still before filling the air with the stench of sulfur.

"Will!" Bee cried, kneeling beside him and taking his hand in hers.

He nodded as he slumped back against the chair with a sigh.

I took a steadying breath, adrenaline still pounding through my veins as I peered around Dom to take stock of the young prince. He was still pale, and his jaw looked painfully unhinged, but he was alive.

It hadn't gone exactly like I'd imagined, but I would count it as a win. I slumped against Dom's back, my body trembling.

Lycan and Loch dealt with the remains of the worm as the Duchess first tipped a goblet of blood down Will's gullet, then worked to free him from his chains.

"You're going to have to reset your jaw, my boy. But you did well. Brave as any king, indeed. Edmund wishes he had your fortitude."

"Aye. Too bad we didn't put the thing in a jar so we could stuff it down the bastard's throat," Loch growled.

"Are you alright, Starshine?" Dom asked, turning until he faced me, his gaze scanning me from head to toe as if to reassure himself I was still whole and hearty.

"I am. No harm done."

Other than the fact that I was losing my mind, of course. I'd been speaking the God's honest truth when I'd told Bee I couldn't connect with non-sentient creatures, but here I was getting life advice from a worm. I briefly considered telling the others what had happened, but then opted to keep it to myself. If I was going insane, I needed to come to terms with it on my own before spreading the word. Besides, we'd all been through enough this day already, and it wasn't even noon.

Dominic's gaze had left my face and had travelled down

to my bloodied hand. There was no hiding the want in his eyes, or the sudden bolt of need that coursed through me seeing it. But he just circled my wrist with his fingers and tugged the towel from my unresisting hand to press it against my wound.

"Nicky, there's no point staunching the flow," the Duchess said, the note of pity in her voice unmistakable. "I know it's difficult, but William needs her blood if he is to heal quickly."

Dominic looked like he wanted to argue, but I shook my head.

"We need us all to be strong and in full health if we have any chance to win this war."

And I wasn't sure we stood a chance even then.

Reluctantly, he released me and stepped aside. I made my way toward Will, who had already reset his jaw and was rotating it left and then right. As I pulled the towel from my hand, Will held up one finger and turned to Bee.

"Gods be merciful, I cannot thank you enough, Bethany. You are a true friend, and I'm amazed at your brilliance. Tell me, what boon can I offer for your service to the crown?"

She blinked up at him from her perch at his feet and then

she rose, as if it were she who was royalty.

"You can go fuck yourself, Will."

With that, she turned and rushed headlong out of the room, slamming the door behind her.

The sound echoed through the room long after she'd left until, finally, the Duchess let out a long-suffering sigh.

"Apparently, bloodworms eat brains as well. Who knew?"

CHAPTER 4

Dominic

My head buzzed like a nest of hornets as I shouldered the door of the keep open and plowed through. After my sparring session with Will, I'd searched out Loch and the two of us had drunk enough to fell men three times our size, but the alcohol didn't even touch the need threatening to incinerate me from the inside out. It was as if it were alive, and almost as agonizing as my time under the full heat of the sun that had all but consumed me.

My long strides ate up the stone floor as I marched passed the corridor to Sienna's quarters without stopping.

She couldn't have made it any clearer. She didn't want me.

Correction.

She didn't *want* to want me. And somewhere along the line, I'd stopped prioritizing my needs over hers. If my presence caused her pain, then I would stay away, even if it killed me.

I reached my bedroom door and the memory of her scent wrapped around me like a shroud. I groaned as my whole body tensed.

Another correction.

It wasn't a question of if it killed me. It was only a question of when.

"Gods be damned," I muttered, debating whether to suffer alone in my bed or head back to the pub for more drink. Tomorrow marked the full moon, though, and already, the wolves were getting restless. There had been a number of brawls that I'd managed to keep my nose out of, but it had been a close thing. The way I was feeling right now, I wouldn't be able to resist the mayhem, if only to work off some of the heat in my blood, and Loch wouldn't even be there to talk sense into me this time. The last thing I needed was to make enemies here.

I shoved the door open and moved to enter but stopped short, sniffing the air.

Not a memory. It was reality. Sienna had been here.

I poked my head into the room and scanned the area, my gaze lighting on the massive bed.

And there she was. My own Sleeping Beauty, one arm

tucked under her head, clutching my pillow close to her face.

My knees nearly buckled, and I held onto the door frame for purchase.

Had she known how badly I'd needed her right now? Or was she there because she needed me too?

I couldn't be sure, and it didn't matter. All that mattered was that she was here.

But lord, was she beautiful. The sheets had slipped down, leaving her mostly visible. She wore a nightgown with slim straps and a lace hem that skimmed the top of her thighs. The pressure in my gums built in tandem with the pressure behind my zipper.

Take it easy, big guy. Your woman needs her rest.

Making as little noise as possible, I stripped off my clothes, down to my skivvies. I almost took those off too, but I was only a vampire, made of flesh and blood, and feeling her skin to skin, head to toe?

Sleep would be out of the question for either of us.

I climbed into the bed, and she instantly rolled closer, curling into me. The number of women, vampires and humans alike, numbered in the hundreds of the many long years of my life, and in that moment, I could remember none of them. I don't know how long we laid there like that, her warm, soft body flush with mine as I held her tight, letting her very presence soothe my soul. But I knew when things changed. Felt her nipples harden like pebbles, branding my chest through the silky nightgown. Hissed when she pressed her hips closer, flexing them against mine. Heard the soft catch of her breath as I tightened my grip on her hip.

"Starshine?" I murmured softly, making sure I was right and that she was awake.

Gods save me, let her be a-fucking-wake.

"Yes," she whispered in a puff of breath against my neck.

"I'm glad you're here," I replied simply.

There was so much more I wanted to say, but the words died in my throat as she closed a small, soft hand around my rigid cock.

"I'm glad too," she said, a smile in her voice.

In that moment, I almost wanted to pull away just to see it. How long had it been since I'd seen her smile? But as she began to move her hand, stroking me, working my shaft up and down through the thin cotton that separated us, my brain went up in flames.

"Ah, you feel good, love," I muttered, sliding a hand

between us to cup her breast.

She gasped wordlessly, arching into me as I pinched her nipple between my thumb and forefinger. And suddenly, the pretty nightgown that looked so sexy on her became nothing but a barrier between the two of us.

I curled my fingers around one of the straps and tugged hard. It gave with a snap. Slowly, like I was unwrapping a gift, I slipped the silky fabric down. Her busy hand froze when the material caught on her nipple, and I could hear the pulse in her neck stutter.

How much did I want to lean down and sink my teeth in? Just a taste...just one sip—

I let out a growl and rolled onto my back in one blazingly swift motion, carrying her with me.

"Oh!" She blinked down at me, clearly surprised to find herself astride me as if I was the horse and she was my rider. "Oh," she whispered again as she leaned into her new circumstance, spreading her legs wider to accommodate me. The second she did it, I knew she wasn't wearing panties. The scent of her pussy filled my head—sweet and juicy—and it was almost my undoing.

"I want to taste you," I muttered, already gripping her waist to lift her to my mouth.

But Sienna had other plans.

"Not yet. I want you inside me."

Her golden eyes swirled with need as she shimmied her shoulders and sent the top of her nightgown sliding down to pool at her hips. She ground against me, and I let out a low growl as my cock bucked.

She reached between us and tugged it free. Then, she held my gaze as she lowered herself onto me, inch by excruciating inch.

"So wet. So fucking tight," I grunted, balls already aching with the need to come.

At my wit's end, I reached between us and thumbed her slick clit, working it in light, gentle circles.

"Not fair," she said, her breath catching as she bounced on my cock, slow and easy at first, and then with a purpose.

It was like something out of a dream watching her. White teeth clamped down on that full bottom lip, hair wild around her shoulders, tits bouncing with those rose-tipped nipples just begging for my mouth.

"Sienna," I growled. It was a warning. When had I become this male? The one who lacked any control?

But the question blew away like smoke as she moved faster. A woman possessed, riding me harder, hips slapping against mine.

"Yes," she whispered, cupping her breasts, pinching her nipples, leaning forward to take me deeper.

My head hummed even as my fangs popped free. This woman was perfect. This woman was everything.

"You want that cock? Take it, Starshine. Take what you want from me," I urged, my dick swelling to the point of pleasure pain.

Her hips were wild now as I worked that sweet little button.

"Come for me, love."

She stiffened suddenly and then froze. "Dom!"

A second later, all hell broke loose. Her silky channel squeezed so tight, I wanted to howl...Gripping me, milking me even as she screamed her own release.

I gripped her hips tight and worked her spasming body over my cock once, twice—

"Fuck!" I snarled as I exploded inside her, hot liquid pulsing from me in waves.

It went on forever and still, it was over too soon.

I closed my eyes to relish the last of her tremors as she collapsed against my chest, spent.

"Thank you."

I could barely hear her with her lips against my neck and I pulled back slightly.

"I should be thanking you," I replied, stroking her back, dewy with sweat. "What a nice surprise to find you here. I thought—"

It didn't matter what I thought. Nothing mattered except that she was here with me, now.

She rolled to my side, leaving one leg hooked over mine as she stroked my chest idly.

"Dom...I'm sorry," she whispered into the darkness. "I'm so sorry."

"I'm sorry too," I said, pulling her closer. "For everything you've been through, and for anything I've done to have a hand in that. You've been through so much."

"And most of that isn't your fault, but I took it out on you. Sometimes I just get so angry. Why is life so unfair?"

She was right, and it was something that had vexed me for more than a century. I wished I had an answer for her, but all I could do was hold her.

We stayed that way for a long time, but eventually, her breathing went soft, and she fell asleep in my arms. Finally at peace. She'd been so angry that I'd let myself burn to save her, I wonder how mad she would be if she knew the whole truth;

That I'd have burned down the entire world if I had to.

Chapter 5

Sienna

"Friend, indeed," Bee mumbled as she finished making her bed.

It had been nearly twenty-four hours ago, and she hadn't stopped talking about it since.

"And then he offers me the fucking crown's gratitude? Have you ever heard of something so stupid?"

I hummed in agreement for the hundredth time. She was dead right. Will had behaved like a real asshole, and as Bee's ride or die, I wasn't about to point out that he'd just had a demon worm the size of a large house cat exorcised from his body out his mouth hole.

Because that wasn't what friends did.

Besides, Bee wasn't the only one behaving irrationally these days. We'd all had our moments...

My thoughts turned to Dom, and I swiftly pushed them away.

"Men are thick. There's no getting around it. All I can

say is that he was right about one thing. You truly saved the day, Bee. Maybe even the whole Empire."

But most importantly, to her at least, she'd saved Will. And despite her griping, I could tell she was relieved to the core that he wasn't dead.

Even if she *did* want to kill him right now.

"It was a team effort. Your blood brought him back to full health, which is just as important as anything I did."

Bee had already stormed out, overwrought and hurt, so I had filled her in when I came to bed as she hadn't been there to witness it.

But Dom had.

Feeding Will, despite him not touching me at all this time, had never felt so intimate and weird. With Dominic there, though, I couldn't wait for it to be over. It felt...wrong. Like I was giving Will something that belonged to his brother.

Don't be pathetic. People don't belong *to other people, you ninny.*

"Well, I refuse to spend the rest of my day thinking about that idiot of a man-child," Bee said with an indignant sniff. "I'm going down to help Loch feed the kraken and then I'm going to help *myself* to a full English breakfast before

I go get more weapons from the armory to sharpen, if you want to join me?"

I thanked her for the invite but shook my head. "I've got some things to take care of here. I'll see you down at the courtyard in an hour or so."

She tossed a wave over her shoulder and headed out the door.

That was good. I'd been hoping to get some time alone to head down to Diana's study and check out some of her books. Surely, there had to be some information somewhere about talking worms. Not to mention all the terrifying thoughts that had plagued me all night long.

What if I didn't have what it took to control my power?

What if, soon, I'd only be able to hear the thoughts of creatures around me, but not my own?

What if I was sliding down a slippery slope into madness, heading for a freefall?

"Diana stopped me on my way out," Bee said, poking her head around the open door less than a minute later. "She and the Oracle want to see you in her study."

Myrr had been staying at the keep since Diana had first sent for her. She hadn't been much help unless you counted emptying the larders as a help.

"Thanks," I murmured, taking a moment to put my hair up before yanking on my vest.

I veered off to grab a sweet bun from the kitchens before heading to meet with Diana. Despite the pillowy softness and the sweet glaze that normally made my mouth water, I took one bite and could barely swallow it.

Grieving Jordan was going to be a long, intense process that I was not looking forward to.

The door was open, so I stepped into the study without knocking and tossed my bun into the trash can.

"Have you lost your mind?" Myrr demanded, shooting up from her seat far more quickly than her gnarled, ancient body should have been able to.

I didn't answer because, frankly, I'd just been wondering the same thing.

She hitched her way over to the can and plucked the bun out, pausing to inspect it with one, milky eye. "Five second rule."

I wanted to mention that the five second rule was traditionally applied to the floor, not the garbage, but Diana pursed her lips and said nothing, so I followed suit.

"Sienna...you look tired," the Queen said as Myrr happily munched on her bun, smacking her lips as she chewed.

"Not sleeping will do that to a girl," I chirped, taking a seat next to the Oracle.

Diana's brows caved in with a concerned frown. "We've got to make sure that you are well rested and feeling strong. Your health is every bit as important as William's, if not more so. I take it you have no appetite either?" she added, jerking a chin to the mostly eaten treat Myrr was demolishing.

"It's been a tough time, but I'll get it together. I just need a second to regroup."

A second to box up all this devastation and fear and tuck it away, to take out and open a long time from now so it could destroy me then instead of now, when the fate of the world depended on me being okay.

"Have you been able to connect to the Hunters at all?"

A question she posed three times daily, if not more often, and one that, since Jordan's death, I hadn't been able to answer the way she wanted.

"No. I can sense them vaguely, but nothing concrete."

The Oracle nodded, pausing to lick her fingers. "I've been there before."

"But you've had some success lately," Diana reminded

her. "As have you, Sienna. We just need you to take care of yourself so we can—"

"Yeah, I know. So, you can use me for intel." She had the weight of an entire people on her, so it probably wasn't fair, but again, I wasn't in a fair kind of mood.

The Queen lifted one shoulder and nodded slowly. "Among other things."

Hey, at least she was honest.

"Is that why you summoned me? To tell me to eat my veggies and get some vitamin D?"

"I summoned you because we want to get to the root of your magic in hopes that we can learn more about it. Its origins, how to control it...hone it. Who are your people, Sienna?"

"My people?" I sat back and crossed my arms over my chest. "Joe and Lurlene Baxter. My dad was a plumber, my mom was a waitress, and by the end, they hated each other's guts."

But I couldn't deny, they'd loved me. As best they could, at least. Still, if there was one thing I was sure of it was that they were as mundane as they came.

"And after they died?"

"I was sent to a distant cousin of my father's in England.

She found me difficult and too willful and sent me to the orphanage."

Diana's eyes filled with pity and something like understanding. "It's hard to feel unwanted."

"Right," I said, forcing a tight smile. "I'll make a note to talk to my therapist about it. Look, I don't want to be an asshole here, but I'm not sure how any of this is going to help…"

"We cannot predict the future without exploring the past," Myrr said softly.

It wasn't a prophecy, but that didn't make her words any less true.

"Okay, then," I said with a weary sigh. "Fire away."

"At the orphanage, before the explosion, was it a happy place?" Diana asked.

"It was as happy as a place like that could be."

I thought back to it for real for the first time in years. To soft-spoken Mistress Deitz who would gently braid my long, blonde locks. To the kindly cook Maurice who would sneak me hand pies when no one was looking because he knew how I loved them. To my friend Rose, who I'd shared a room with until that fateful day.

"You mentioned your hair changed color. When did that

happen?" Diana pressed, studying me carefully.

"About a month after the explosion. Maybe it was earlier than that, but that's when it became really noticeable. The doctors there felt it was likely due to trauma."

"Do you?" Myrr asked, leaning forward in her chair.

"I don't really know because I didn't feel traumatized. Not consciously, at least. I don't recall most of it, to be honest. I just remember being outside during recess, running around the stone pillars with a group of girls. We were playing hide and seek. The skies went dark and there was this sound—"

I broke off as my heart began to race.

"Then, nothing. The next thing I knew, I was in the hospital. One of my eardrums burst, and I'd hit my head but other than that, I was fine."

Except the nightmares. They'd lasted for years. I could never quite hold onto them when I woke, though. I just knew they were bad.

Real bad.

"How old were you then?"

"Five. Nearly six."

"Fifteen years ago, then?" Myrr asked, glancing toward

Diana pointedly.

"Yes, exactly."

"The same time that the Veil fell."

"I don't think it was," I replied, squinting as I thought back. "It was months before that."

"It was months before you *humans* knew it had fallen," Diana corrected. "We knew immediately and used everything in our arsenal to stay hidden. Fae and angels working together to keep us from sight until we could repair what had been broken. But alas, it was not to be."

"So, you think the explosion has something to do with the Veil falling?" I asked in disbelief. By all accounts it was a localized event. One that made news in London but nowhere else. Surely, it would've taken more than that to break the Veil.

"I can't say for sure, but it's a theory. I'm going to get my tech team to research it and see what they can find out. They're also working on some stealth drones to locate and follow the Hunters, undetected. In the meantime, let's see if we can start honing your powers to make them more useful. Learning to connect and even control other creatures at will could be the difference in winning and losing this war."

Diana stood and waved for Myrr and I to follow. She led us out to the courtyard, where Lochlin and several others were training.

"Lochlin, we need you for a few moments," she called.

A few minutes later, the three of us stood under the shade of an elm tree as Diana stood before us.

"Lochlin, if you please, shift to your wolf form for us."

Without question, Lochlin inclined his head and did as instructed. One moment, he was a burly, ginger-haired man, the next, he was a burly, ginger wolf.

Huzzah for me that it no longer even fazed me.

"Sienna. See if you can connect with Loch's wolf," Diana encouraged as the animal loped in tight circles around us.

"Alright." Nerves fluttered in my belly.

I closed my eyes and breathed deep through my nose, opening my consciousness to the creatures around me. Loch's presence was closest and a strong energy, so I latched on easily.

Hello, my friend.

He paused and cocked his head at me.

Friend, he confirmed, his wolfy lips almost grinning at me.

"I can hear him," I whispered, trying to speak and stay aware of my surroundings while maintaining the connection rather than slipping into that weird trance like I had with the kraken.

"See if you can force him to change back to human form," Diana said, eyes narrowed as she watched intently.

I swallowed hard and pressed deeper into the wolf's mind, past his thoughts, all the way to his will.

I could feel Loch trying to pull away from me even as his wolf form began to pant.

"Sienna, until we know what you can do, we—"

I broke the connection with Lochlin and stumbled backward against the tree behind me.

"Just because I *can* do something, doesn't mean I should, Your Majesty. I won't do what you ask. Not to someone who has been a friend to me."

Not when I myself had been forced, time and time again over the past weeks, to do things against my will, hating every fucking second of it.

Diana studied me for a long moment and then nodded. "I understand, and I can respect that. So let us compromise. For the good of the masses, both here and on the mainland, would you be willing to try to impose your will on a crow or falcon? The bird won't be harmed. We just need it to do some recon. That is all."

I considered her request and found I couldn't say no. While it still didn't feel right to take over another creature's mind, Diana was right. The ends justified the means.

"I can try."

It wound up being a whole lot easier than I'd ever imagined. Not only was I able to enlist the help of a pair of crows to become our eyes in the sky, I also sent the kraken on a mission to Blackthorne Harbor to monitor the seas.

While it had been a successful morning by all accounts, by the end of it, I was drained. Spent to the point that I could barely stand.

"We thank you for all your service, Sienna. You've been a tremendous help."

A stab of guilt hit me. The words from the worm, they were still haunting me.

"I should probably tell you something else, in the vein of being helpful."

I quickly filled them in on the voice I'd heard coming from the worm, which sent Myrr into a tizzy.

"That sounds like black magic to me. Diana and I will do our best to get to the bottom of it while you eat, rest and regain your strength."

The two women headed off, leaving me alone with Loch, who had shifted back to his human form.

"Yer pretty amazing, Lass," he said, shaking his head in awe. "But even more than that, yer a good woman. I appreciate ye not using me like some sort of marionette, I do."

He yanked me into a bear hug and I let out an *oof* and a chuckle.

"No problem."

I returned his hug, glad for it in that moment. Because, despite being surrounded by people pretty much all the time, none of them were like me, and I couldn't remember the last time I'd felt so alone...

CHAPTER 6

Dominic

I followed the faintest trace of Sienna's scent through the halls, though I didn't truly need to. I knew that Diana had wanted to talk to her about her powers, to see what Sienna could do.

I couldn't help the way my hands tightened into fists. Diana, of course, had seen fit to send me off with General Baran Whalen rather than be a part of Sienna's little training session. Admittedly, the time spent with the General was important, preparing for war was no small thing. It was the right way to spend my time. I'd been in several wars, and they had a feel to them before the worst of the battles struck. A tension, a growing weight at the base of the skull, while every animalistic part of the body told you to run, and your mind prevailed and bade you stay.

We were in the thick of that weight, of that humming push to flee or fight.

The truth of it though was, I wanted nothing more but

to bury myself in Sienna, to push the world away.

For the first time in my long life, I would have rather not fought, given the choice.

I reached the hall that led to Diana's chambers, voices touching the edges of my hearing.

"*Yer pretty amazing lass.*"

Lochlin then was there with them, that was good. Keeping a guard near her at all times was important still. He was a good friend.

The door was not closed tight, and I pushed it open a few inches.

Sienna enclosed in Lochlin's brawny arms; his head bent to touch her shoulder was not what I expected.

Like a horse kick to the head, I stood there stunned for the space of a single second, the world spinning and tightening to the view of just them, then I turned and strode away.

Not because I thought anything was happening, quite the opposite. I knew Lochlin...he would never. And I knew Sienna...But the animal part of me?

Wanted to fucking tear his head off for even touching her when I was unable to, and if I stayed, I wasn't sure how I'd behave. I'd damaged our friendship already on this trip,

I didn't need to do it again based off what was surely an innocent hug.

The growl that escaped me was impossible to catch. Gods be damned.

First, Sienna fed Will, and not that it was intimate at all between them, but the sharing of blood was a bonding act no matter how it was done. No matter that it was to save Will's life there would always be a connection between them.

Then to see her in Loch's arms? Too much for my overwrought...feelings? No, it was more than just feelings, it was as if my body knew through to the marrow of me that she belonged in my arms and seeing her in his was shaking me to the literal core.

I flared my nostrils, two wolves sidled past me, one of them shaking his head.

"Poor bastard."

The growl that rumbled out of my chest would have made any wolf proud and they just kept on moving.

My strides took me out of the keep and into the main training yard. This was where I'd left General Whalen, and I was looking for a good spar. He was gone, but even better, Will stood on the edge of the yard, looking like the image of health and vitality.

Because of Sienna.

"Will. Sparring. Now." I snapped each word as I shrugged out of my vest and tossed it to the side. I went straight for the weapons lined up against the wall.

My fingers found the only ironwood staff, the feel of it shimmering against my fingertips. I grabbed it and tossed it to Will. "You're going to need this."

"Feeling wound up, are we?"

The laughter in his voice grated at me and I found myself pulling not one, but two swords.

I snarled as I swung the right sword, pivoted on my right foot and swung the left sword like an uppercut.

Will caught the swords easily.

Which was why I had tossed him the ironwood staff and I'd taken swords. They were not my strong suit, and I didn't need to be cutting Will up, even though he'd drank from my mate.

I lunged toward him, at the last second jumping up and bringing both swords down.

Will drove the tip of the ironwood into my gut and sent me flying backward.

"Sloppy, brother," he said with a pitying *snick* of his

tongue. "What has your panties in a wad today? Wait, let me guess..."

I gasped trying to catch my breath. "Fuck you."

"Succinct, but I do believe it is the fact that she *isn't* fucking you that's got you all wound into a knot of grumpy pants?"

He spun the staff, and the low hum of the ironwood filled the air. I moved with him, looking for my opening. But he was...different. Faster, lighter on his feet than he'd ever been, and I knew why.

Her blood. The curses on the tip of my tongue were nothing to the rage that snapped through me, his taunts fueling the anger that I couldn't deny. My two blades came down across the ironwood, one after the other, then I ducked and stood up inside Will's guard, the staff behind me.

His eyes were wide as I snapped my head forward, catching him on the bridge of the nose and sending him stumbling away.

"Fuck, Dom, you broke my nose, you asshole!" Will turned and faced me, blood dripping down his face. He dropped the ironwood and grabbed both sides of his nose and twisted hard, resetting it.

I was still breathing hard, still wanting to fight, but not wanting to hurt him. I turned to the training dummy and laid into it with both swords until one snapped. Then with a scoop of my toe I pulled the ironwood staff to me and began to work through the motions that settled me like nothing else could.

From behind me, Will called out the movements, the humming staff warming in my hand.

"Moonfall to sunrise."

My staff connected with the side of the dummy's head, then I swept it down across the legs.

"Mule-kick to shattered trees."

I drove the butt of the staff into the dummy's gut, then spun and whipped it across the ribs.

"Dancing monkey to love-starved vampire."

I stopped in my movements and turned to see a grinning Will laughing at me, his face and eyes sparking with more health and vitality than I'd ever seen in him. "What the fuck did you just say?"

He leaned against a tree, watching me casually. "You like that one? I thought you'd know it well, seeing as you are at least one half of the equation."

"And the dancing monkey?" I growled.

"Oh good, see I was worried you wouldn't recognize that you were a love-starved vampire."

I grimaced, sweat running down my body as I finally took a slow breath, the anger and frustration flowing away from me.

None of this was anyone's fault.

"Walk with me, brother." Will motioned for me to join him. Another heavy sigh and I slid the ironwood back into the stack of staffs.

"You are fully healed?" Yes, I went for the easier topic.

Will laughed. "You want to start here? Sure. Yes, I am fully healed. In fact, I don't think I've ever felt this good. If it hadn't been for Bethany, I would be dead. And you'd be fighting Edmund for the throne."

I shook my head. "No. I would have killed him still, but I have no aspirations to be king."

Yes, this was safer territory than—

"Of course, if not for Sienna's blood, Bethany would never have had the time to come up with the solution. I'd have been long dead."

The anger wasn't there this time, more resignation.

"Can you sense her?"

Will shot a look at me before shrugging. "Distantly, I

guess. It isn't the same connection as I'd expect. I can tell what direction she is roughly, but not her feelings or what she's doing. Not like a true human feeder."

That was interesting.

Will cleared his throat. "I also think that if she called me, I would...have to go to her. I'm not sure that the blood bond with her works like any I've experienced in the past."

I shot a look at him. "She can control you?"

"I don't know that I'd go that far, but I feel protective of her, more than before. Like family, if that makes sense. I've always found her funny as hell, and sharp as the point of your swords but this is like...like she's a sister. More than Diana, in some ways." He shrugged. "Nothing like how I feel about Bethany."

We were at the edge of the water, the ocean sliding back and forth over the sand. Even with the kraken gone to spy on Blackthorne Harbor, the boats were not many on the water.

I looked at my brother, truly looked, and saw the same sorrow that I was dealing with—a woman he was afraid to love, afraid to hold tight.

"We could all die tomorrow," I said.

Will startled and looked across at me. "True."

"So why are you not holding Bethany tight while you can? Regrets are not something you can afford, Will. By all rights you should be dead, and yet you're alive. You have another chance at this thing called life." I paused. "Live it as you wish, the crown be damned. Fuck her, hell, bite her, mark her as your own in every way you can, for tomorrow is not given to any of us. Especially now."

Will grunted. "Pot, meet kettle. Oh, lovely to meet you, you hypocritical ass."

My lips twitched upward. "I know."

I did know. I knew exactly why I was so wrought up, outside of the blood sharing and Lochlin hugging Sienna. I knew that tomorrow could be our last, or the day after, and I hated believing that there would be no more moments with Sienna.

That I would regret so much.

"How are you holding up with Scarlett turning on us? Do you think it's for real, or just an act to save her skin while she is with him?"

Will's words dug into the other thorn that was festering in my side.

"She's with him." I shook my head. "I saw her eyes; I know her and she...I have seen her eyes when she hates someone and doesn't hold back. I never thought I'd see it directed at me. That she would go so far as to side with Edmund."

More than that, it had been Scarlett's arrow that had killed Jordan, and set Sienna against me once more. Only this time I wasn't sure I could convince her that I would have done everything I could to protect the boy. That I hadn't known. I ran my hands through my hair, hating Scarlett, perhaps as much as she hated me right now. She had cost me the one person that I loved.

I swallowed hard, still unable to fully come to terms with it.

Will grunted. "She's been trained by you, how much of an issue is that going to be in the upcoming battle?"

I nodded, grateful for the change of direction. "She knows how my mind works; she will likely be able to guess at the strategy that I look to employ. We need to make choices that will be unpredictable, that will keep them wondering what direction we are taking. I taught Scarlett so that she would be ready to take my place as a general should I fall."

Will smiled. "But that means you know how she thinks…what she will do too, correct?"

I snorted. "Do I? Because I surely had not seen her betrayal coming. Not for all the money in the world would I have bet that she'd turn to Edmund's side, not after all the evil she'd seen in him. And I cannot wrap my brain around the why of it. Was it because I left her behind? I had no choice, she had to know that I'd never have done it given any ability to do otherwise."

"Let me enlighten you, brother. You were fucking Scarlett, were you not?"

I blinked and looked over at him. "Yes. But that was an arrangement that—"

"I can guarantee you it was not *that* for her. There were rumors, of course, just rumors. But Bethany was very good at having her ear to the ground in the castle. Scarlett fully expected you to take her as a mate at some point if the rumblings were to be believed."

Well fuck.

"So, she thought that Sienna was taking her place?"

"Not thought, brother. We both know the truth. Sienna had your heart the moment you saw her at that auction, the same way that Bethany had mine the first night she stepped into the Harvest Games. And we've both been doing all we can to protect them. The difference is, I wasn't fucking an apparent sociopath with high levels of warfare training that I cast off in order to chase the woman my heart wanted."

Ouch.

"The sociopath will be dealt with," I assured him, the rage I felt toward Scarlett still burning bright in my chest.

Will clapped a hand on my shoulder and gave me a squeeze. "The end game is coming, brother. And we both have things to do." He turned away from me and headed for the castle.

"Where are you going?" I called after him.

"You're right. We could die tomorrow. I don't want to regret anything. And neither should you."

I watched my brother go, jogging up the beach toward the keep.

I followed him, slower. Not because I also wouldn't have liked to spend the night with the only woman I wanted.

The only problem? She most certainly did not want me at the moment.

CHAPTER 7

Sienna

Sleep and the supposed respite it brought, was not my friend at the moment. I'd gone to bed early after the attempt at commanding Lochlin to obey me. Even though I'd backed off and not pushed my will on his, I could feel the truth under my skin.

I could have done it.

I could have forced him to bend to me, and there would have been no choice on his part. He would have been my slave, even though he had a mind of his own. The animal in him wanted to obey me more than it wanted to obey him.

And that bloody well terrified me.

I rolled to my side, the blankets hot and twisting around me. I opened my eyes to stare into the darkness, only it wasn't darkness I saw.

Jordan stood in front of me, bare chested, pale as if he had no blood left in him, the wound near his heart gaping, drip lines of black blood running down his narrow chest.

"Ceecee, you said you'd protect me. That I'd be safe. You said you'd come for me. But you didn't. You didn't do what you said you would."

I moaned as I reached for him. "Jordan, I tried. I came here for you. I wanted to take you away, like I said—"

"No, you didn't try, you were too slow. Just like before. When the Collectors took me, you were too slow then, too." His eyes were angry and sad. But sadder than anything else.

Disappointed.

His gaze was an arrow, piercing me in a way nothing else could have.

Shaking, I stood up and went to him, holding out my hands. Taking his ice-cold, dead fingers in my own, holding him tight, as if I could even now save him.

"Jordan, please. I didn't want you to die, I wanted to save you! I love you, Jordan, you know that, please, you must know that everything I've done, I did to find you."

He took a step back, putting space between us, shaking his head as he stared at me. *"So many promises you didn't keep. If you really loved me, you would have tried harder. You would have saved me."*

His words were sharper than any hair pin going straight

through my heart, and I went to my knees, legs buckling as I stared up at him, tears streaming down my face. "No, I came for you, Jordan, I came for you!"

"If you'd left, I wouldn't be dead. I'd be alive."

The sobs were heavy in my chest as I shook my head. "No, no. Jordan that's not true."

His gaze was heartless, cold and angry as he jerked his hands from mine. *"You were warned that we'd all die, and you stayed."*

Shaking, I wrapped my arms around myself, trying to ward off the bite and cold of the words that were cutting me to pieces. Words from the boy that had been my only family for years. Words from the boy that I loved enough to throw my own life into the fire to save.

Blinking, I looked up at him and for just a split second the image wavered. Jordan's body was superimposed over another. A cloaked figure, long hair flowing from under the hood, feminine curves. Indistinct. But there, nonetheless.

I shook my head and slowly pushed to my feet. This dream was a dream, but it was real too. Impossibly real even if I didn't understand it. "You aren't Jordan, are you?"

His body slid away, and I was left staring at the cloaked and hooded woman. She was taller than me, and though she was curvy she was solid too.

Her voice was husky, and it was the same voice I'd heard from the worm, and from the dream of the daisies. "You were warned. You failed to heed my warning, and you paid the price."

I stiffened my spine and glared at her. I was sure this was the bitch who killed Jordan, as much as Scarlett. "Who are you?"

Her laughter spun out, all around me. "I am everything, I am the world, I am the stars and the darkness, you should bow before me, grateful to be in my presence."

There was pressure on my legs, pushing me back to my knees and I pushed back. "You killed Jordan, didn't you?" I couldn't even say how I knew, I only felt it in my gut, and my gut was rarely wrong.

I couldn't see her smile, but her glee was palpable. "I made sure it happened, yes. To make a point. You cannot stop me; you cannot stop what is coming."

She thrust a hand toward my heart, palm facing me, dagger like claws on the ends of her fingers and flexed them. The pain that shot through me was immediate, lancing outward from the tips of her fingers, sliding through to the marrow of my bones. Electricity from her touch slammed into me, arching my back, and exposing my throat.

I screamed and she laughed, but the dream didn't let up. I didn't wake from the pain, just writhed in it, tried to find a way to stop it, but there was no way. I was caught.

I struggled to breathe.

"Perhaps I can kill you now? You are rather weaker than I expected, *Corumbra*. It seems Elhimna chose poorly." Her hand snapped out and she slapped me hard, knocking me sideways to the ground.

I managed a breath. "Fuck. You."

My mind whirled and my energy dipped, but my power slipped out around me, searching for something. Searching for a rope with which to pull myself up with.

I latched onto an animal without thought and drew from them. A pair of hawks sitting outside my window, as if they were watching over me. They gave their power freely, though one fell from the ledge, giving his life to save mine.

Using the renewed strength, I jerked myself out of the dream and away from the cloaked figure.

Soaked with sweat, I lay flat on my back breathing hard as if I'd been truly in a fight for my life. But it was just a dream, wasn't it? I looked out the window in time to see a single bird take flight, though it struggled with the first few beats of its wings, it did fly away. The other was gone.

So, it wasn't just a dream?

I lifted a hand and touched my face, feeling the heat and imprint of a hand. Fear shot through me, and I struggled out of the blankets and to my feet.

"Sienna?" Bethany spoke softly from her side of the room. "Are you okay? You've been moaning in your sleep."

"I...just bad dreams."

"I can't sleep either." The light bloomed as she flicked it on and rolled out of bed. "Do you want something to eat?"

I didn't, but I nodded. "Please."

She slipped out of the room, leaving me alone, and I instantly regretted that she was gone.

The shadows seemed to creep closer, even with the light on, as if they were alive and stalking me. As if the cloaked woman was there, waiting for me to lay down my guard.

What was happening to me? Despite the conversation I'd had with the Oracle and Diana, they didn't know why I would hear a voice from the worm, or what might be happening inside my head.

And the cloaked woman had called me Corumbra. What did that mean? And who was Elhimna?

Too many questions, and no answers.

I touched my cheek again, feeling the heat there. Wobbling a little, I went to the mirror and stared at my reflection.

The imprint had the tips of claws at the end of the fingers and was clearly visible. I swallowed hard.

Bethany stepped back into the room with a crystal decanter of dark amber liquid. "Forget food, we need booze. That will help us sleep eventually."

I turned and she looked straight at me, her eyes going to my cheek. "What the hell is that?"

Shaky, I walked to her bed and sat on the edge. "Good question. I think I'm losing it, Bee. I...I had a dream and this terrible woman tried to kill me, then she slapped me, and I woke up with this."

"How scary!" Bethany pressed a gentle hand to my face. "She's a big girl, her hand is far larger than mine."

Tears pooled in the corner of my eye. She didn't think I was crazy. "You believe me."

"Hard to deny what's right in front of me." She poured

me a drink. "Here, you need this."

I sipped the drink, what at first, I would have thought was whiskey, but instead it was a smooth rum that slid down my throat, hints of coconut on the edge of it.

Bethany didn't sip hers but knocked it back like a shot. "Do you want to sleep in my bed? Maybe that will keep the dreams at bay. Not like either of us have anyone fighting to get between the sheets with us."

The laugh was unexpected. "I think Will would like to be in your sheets, Bee. Even if he is an idiot about everything. You even said you two almost...but then he had an attack of conscience."

She snorted and poured herself another drink. "An attack of stupid, maybe."

I smiled and drained my shot, holding out my glass to her. She filled it to the brim, and I sucked down half of it. Maybe alcohol wasn't the answer, but it was nicely numbing the fear that had chased me out of my dream and into the waking world.

"You need to kick him in the balls," I said. The words were somewhat aggressive—thank you rum shots— "I mean, how can he not wonder if we'll even make it to tomorrow? I could have died tonight in my sleep because of some crazy bitch who has a Voldemort complex! You could die tomorrow, even if we weren't at war. We don't know what the next hour will bring, never mind the next day."

I swallowed a sudden lump in my throat, thinking of Jordan once more. We just didn't know how long we had. At least I'd seen him before he'd died. But that was a cold comfort. And the words of the cloaked woman had stirred it in me. Jordan's death was as much my fault as anyone's. I hadn't gotten to him before the Collectors, if I'd done that, he might not have been killed.

"Right!" Bee snapped back her second shot and poured a third for herself. "We could totally die tomorrow! And then what? Regrets all the way through eternity." She shook her head and took her third shot. "Imma go kick him in the balls, and then offer to kiss the boo boo better."

She slammed down the glass and was off, storming—albeit a little wobbly—out of the room before I could say another word.

"That escalated quickly," I muttered to myself, taking a sip of my rum.

I tried not to think about Jordan, or the woman in the cloak.

We were surrounded by death and the threat of death, by friends and foe and sometimes it was difficult to see where the line was between the two. I emptied the last of my rum and thought about going back to bed alone.

A tremor slid through me. Nope, that was a nope. If Bethany had stayed, I would have taken her up on her offer to sleep in her bed with her. While it wasn't a sure thing that another's presence would keep the dreams at bay, it did make me feel better.

I was pretty sure I could pester Lochlin into letting me be his snuggle 'boog', but it wasn't his arms I needed around me, as a friend or otherwise.

The rum helped me make my decision; I was *quite* sure. But before I changed my mind, I grabbed a silk house robe and wrapped it around me as I left the room. I knew where *his* rooms were. His arms were what I wanted around me.

It didn't take me long to get to the door and I raised my fist to knock, paused, and took a step back. On some sort of weird impulse, I turned around, went back to mine and Bethany's room, and grabbed the bottle of rum.

I made my way back up to his room and knocked on the door with the bottom edge of the bottle. I could tell him to have a drink with me. But after the knock, there was nothing, not a sound.

Was he sleeping?

Or not there?

I turned the handle and pushed the door open. The room was dimly lit, but even so it was immediately apparent that he wasn't there. Closing the door behind me, and setting the rum bottle down on a table, I wandered into the room. Letting my fingers brush over the things that were most certainly his. Leather arm braces, body armor, the ironwood staff he preferred.

Fatigue rolled over me so hard my knees nearly buckled. Sliding out of the silk house coat, I wobbled my way to his bed and slid under the blankets. The pillow smelled like him, and I tucked myself in tight to the scent and feel of Dominic.

Why in the world would his presence keep me safe from the woman in the cloak? I didn't know for sure, but again, it was a gut feeling.

Dominic, no matter where we stood on our feelings for each other, would never let me fight a darkness like that alone. Tears leaked out of my eyes, courtesy of rum and exhaustion. I'd been stupid to push him away, stupid, and childish, and what had it cost me now? The chance at a man that would literally burn himself alive to make sure that I was safe? A man that fought all his base urges to make sure I was okay? He had his flaws, but I could not deny that he was doing his best to protect me. You didn't do that for someone you didn't care about.

"I'm the idiot," I whispered into the pillow, keeping his shirt tucked tight under my cheek.

The blankets were heavy and the fear and worry of the dream, the grief over Jordan, the realization that I may have pushed the man that I not only needed, but wanted more than any other away, weighed me down. Exhaustion, emotional and physical, finally won, and I let sleep take me one more time.

Knowing that here, in Dominic's space, I was safer than I'd ever been in my life.

CHAPTER 8

Sienna

When I awoke the next morning, my body ached in the loveliest way. Lips tender from Dominic's kisses, thighs weak from straining to get closer to him...most of all, though, I felt rested and content. For the first time in I couldn't remember how long, I'd slept through the night. No tossing and turning, no bad dreams, no face-slapping, ghost-bitches. Just pure, unadulterated sleep, and I realized that Diana was right. I needed to take care of myself in order to be as strong as possible for the battle to come. I felt so clear-headed and more able to cope, thank the gods, because I had been one more talking worm incident away from a straitjacket.

Note to self: sleep with Dominic every night...at least, until we all die a horrible death in this war.

I rolled to my side, seeing the empty space where he'd last been lying. I'd known he was already gone from the second my eyes had opened...his presence wasn't something I could miss, but I didn't feel rejected or bereft. If I had questioned his feelings for me, he'd cleared them up last night.

He loved me. It was far from perfect, and I had no idea where it would ultimately lead us—maybe to our doom—but that didn't matter. Not anymore.

We were fated.

Mated.

And there wasn't a damn thing either of us could do about it.

Something about the certainty of that was freeing. There were no decisions to make. No protecting my heart or trying to play it smart. I would follow that path to the bitter end and pay the price it demanded, because I no longer had a choice.

My stomach grumbled and I sat up, stretching.

"Sienna? Are you in there? We need you to come, quickly!"

Diana's voice rang down the hall and I swung my legs over the side of the bed, pulse pounding.

She sounded nervous.

Past nervous.

She sounded scared. The display of emotion was so rare,

it lit a fire under my ass, and I rushed to dress as I called back to her.

"Coming! Be right there!"

I made my way down the hall to find Diana waiting there, face leached of color.

"Something's happened to Bethany," she said without preamble as she clutched my forearm and pulled me toward the opposite corridor. "She was supposed to meet me in the armory early this morning so we could talk through inventory, and she didn't come. It's so unlike her, that I knew something was amiss. Before I could have her summoned, Will came rushing out in a panic."

My heart was in my throat, and I broke into a sprint, Diana hot on my heels. Bee had gone to Will last night, same as I'd gone to Dominic. In fact, I'd encouraged her to do it. Because Will loved her. Surely, he would never have hurt her.

What had Diana said...something about vampires not truly knowing how to love?

I shoved the thought away and burst through Will's bedroom door without knocking.

"What's happened?" I demanded, pausing mid-step in surprise at the number of people in the room.

Lycan and the Duchess by his side, Myrr next to her, and a group of men and women in white lab coats.

"We can't say for sure what's going on, but she's burning up with fever," Evangeline said, waving me forward.

I almost didn't want to go. I hadn't even begun to process the loss of Jordan. If I lost Bee too?

This isn't about you, I reminded myself harshly, forcing my feet into motion.

I closed my eyes and took a deep breath before opening them and peering down at Bethany.

Her face was fire engine red and even as I reached down to lay a hand on her forehead, I could feel the heat pouring off her as she tossed and turned.

"Shh, it's alright, Bee. I'm here," I murmured, laying my icy fingers on her flaming skin.

She hissed in relief, leaning into my touch.

"When did this start?" I demanded, looking to Will, who stood across from me, gaze locked on Bee.

"Half an hour ago, maybe." His nostrils flared and he looked to the ceiling as if hoping it held the answers he was seeking. "She slept fine. I held her through the night, and there was none of this. Then, when the sun came up, it was like—" He broke off, throat working as he tried to continue. "It was like she'd been possessed by a demon. Her body locked up, and she started seizing."

Much the same as Will himself had looked when we'd started luring the bloodworm from his body. But surely...

"Humans can't catch bloodworm, can they? We, I mean," I corrected quickly.

"No, child," Evangeline said, shaking her head slowly. "Bloodworm is named thusly for a reason. It feeds solely on blood ingested into the digestive system. It would die on a diet of mundane foods; therefore, it avoids any host that isn't vampiric."

As much as I didn't relish the thought of excavating another bloodworm from the bowels of a friend, I found myself slightly disappointed. At least we knew we could fix that.

I lifted my hand away, unsurprised to find the chill of my own fear had been melted away by the blistering heat of her skin.

"You're alright," I murmured, laying my other hand on her forehead again and closing my eyes. "I'm right here."

I tried to focus in on that spot deep in my belly, where my power burned brightest, but the second I tried to send its healing properties into Bee, it sizzled away into nothingness.

"Sorry, I just heard," Dominic called, shouldering his way through the team of doctors to take my free hand. "Loch just sent someone to the training grounds to get me. What's happened?"

I wet my lips, gripping his fingers tight, already feeling just a bit steadier at his presence. "We don't know yet."

At that moment, Bee began to toss her head wildly, and made my declaration a lie.

I knew.

The evidence was right there, plain as day, on the creamy skin of her neck, marred by two oozing, crimson holes, blackening around the edges. They looked...wrong.

I stared at Will and tried to keep my voice calm.

"You bit her throat?"

Despite my efforts, it was at once an accusation and a judgement.

It was like I'd forgotten how much I'd wanted Dominic to do that very thing to me just hours before. How close we'd come to sharing this very same intimacy.

"It's not that," Evangeline said before Will could respond. "That doesn't happen."

"She wanted me to," Will said, his expression telling me

we were on the same page despite the Duchess's denial. "She asked me to, but I would never do something to harm her. It shouldn't have affected her in any way except to elicit pleasure. I took so little...I don't understand..." Will shook his head in despair, looking for all the world like a broken man instead of a vampire king.

"It's the truth, Starshine. A simple bite and gentle feeding shouldn't make her sick at all. This would be unprecedented."

And yet, I knew it was so.

"Walk me through how it usually works," I said, turning to face Dominic. "A vampire bites a human, and they feel totally fine afterwards? As if nothing happened?"

"Actually, the science is quite fascinating," one of the male werewolf doctors chimed in, taking the lead. "A chemical is released into the bloodstream that travels to the receptors in the brain. It releases a flood of euphoria, and so much dopamine that it's almost orgasmic. We nearly had an issue with a street drug modeled after that very chemical. Something akin to Molly or Ecstasy in the human realm. We'd have let it slide and called it progress except that it's highly addictive to our kind. We managed to largely eradicate it before it grew to epidemic levels, but

I'm sure there are still a few wolves who create it in their homes for personal use."

"To humans and to other vampires, it does create a drug-like euphoria, but true injury needs to be intended. Like when DuMont scratched you, he went out of his way to mark and hurt you so it would last," Dominic confirmed, lip curling at the memory. "There are no ill-effects other than some soreness in the area as one might expect from a regular wound. At least none that I've ever encountered."

I refused to think about his fangs in someone else's neck during said encounters right now. I needed all my energy focused on figuring out what had happened to Bee and entertaining such a thought would send me down an immature, jealous, rage-filled rabbit-hole from which there was no escape.

Part of me wanted to confirm with Will that he hadn't had a tiny little blip...some moment where all the mess with the possessed bloodworm had maybe caused him to lose his mind temporarily and wish Bethany harm, but one look at his miserable face had me biting my tongue and changing gears.

"And what about turning? A bite has never made a

human into a vamp?" I asked the question by rote even though I already knew the answer.

"Wolves can turn others into our kind, but the same doesn't hold true for them," one of the female doctors said without censure.

"Vampires are born, not made," Evangeline concurred.

"An allergic reaction, then? Maybe to his saliva or?"

I knew I was grasping at straws, because Will had fed from her before, but straws were all I had, and panic was starting to bloom as Bee's body grew inexplicably hotter.

"Again, not something we've seen," Evangeline said with a weary shake of her head. "In fact, Will's saliva should've made the wound almost imperceptible by now. The fact that it's still open like that and oozing is strange in and of itself."

Will took Bee's hand and lifted his head, holding my gaze.

"You saved me more than once, Sienna. Please...can you try again?"

I wanted so much to be some beacon of hope for him, but I stuck with honesty instead.

"I can try. I'll never stop trying, but I don't think it's going to work. It's like there's something inside her working against me. I think we need to start by getting her fever down."

"We've been trying that since the beginning," one of the doctors murmured, gesturing to what looked like a pile of blankets at the foot of the bed. "They're stored in a cryogenic chamber. We had her wrapped in them for the past twenty minutes, and they didn't touch the fever."

"I don't mean to alarm anyone further, but we need to think, and fast if we want all hands-on deck," Diana said, her brow marred with worry. "We have about eight hours before the full moon lights the sky and then we'll be of no help to anyone."

There had been talk of it for the past few days. The wolves had been preparing for the full moon, but I had been too wrapped up in my grief over Jordan to pay much attention to what was going on.

"You'll all need to stay sequestered, and behind locked doors, for your own safety. We take every precaution, and try to keep it as civilized as possible, but I only have so much control once the pull of the moon takes hold. We will be outdoors, largely, but it's very unpredictable. Even the doctors will be...unavailable—"

Suddenly, Bee's eyes popped open, and Diana stopped

short.

Bee grabbed my hand, her nails clawing into my skin. She turned her greedy, fevered gaze to mine and whimpered.

"Please, Sienna...help."

I realized with sickening certainty that it didn't matter what had been true in the past. Will's bite was slowly killing my friend.

And there was nothing I could do to stop it.

CHAPTER 9

Sienna

Time slipped by slow as molasses in February as we sat at Bethany's bedside, her body seeming to break down in front of us. Seven hours and the full moon rose outside, the howls of the packs rippling through the night as their animal selves took over. The only wolves left in the room were Diana and two of the doctors, and even they had taken to growling at us if we moved too quickly. More than once I saw Diana snap her fingers at them, and snarl something under her breath. She had a hold on them.

But just barely.

I reached for the empty glass and pitcher of water on the side table, filled it and then scooted close to Bethany as I'd done so many times in the hours since I'd been sitting with her. "Tip your head up, Bee, I've got water."

She did as I asked and I cupped the back of her head, helping her drink down the entire glass in two gulps.

"More." Her voice sounded parched, as if I'd not just

poured a huge amount of water into her. As if she hadn't drunk gallons and gallons already.

Ignoring the others in the room, I helped her drink until the entire pitcher of water was gone.

"Better?" I smoothed my hand over her face, and nearly hissed. Her skin was so hot, she might as well have been on fire. It was like touching the element of a stove, you didn't burn yourself but only because you jerked away fast enough.

A moan was her only answer as she thrashed her head side to side, her blond hair plastered to her face and neck. The wound was mostly healed now, the evidence of Will's bite all but gone. Surely that was a good sign?

I looked up at Evangeline and asked her the same question that had been asked over and over.

"How do we help her? Duchess, there must be something we can do. I can't believe that in this world of magic there is nothing."

Because I'd tried. I'd tried my healing on her half a dozen times, and I hadn't even been able to connect with her. Because, like Will with the bloodworm, she wasn't truly sick, and she wasn't truly injured.

She was transforming and there wasn't a single thing I

could do to heal that.

We'd even tried feeding her blood, human and vampire and finally a few drops of mine, but she'd choked and gagged, throwing it all up.

Evangeline closed her eyes and slowly shook her head before she looked at me once more. The pain of the sad truth sat within her silver eyes, and it terrified me.

"I do not know how this is even happening, Sienna. Perhaps something to do with the Veil and the seasons, perhaps the very foundations of our magic and existence is changing the longer the Veil is down. There is no precedent for what is happening to our sweet girl, and as such there is nothing to do but make her comfortable for as long as we can."

Make her comfortable. Because she was dying and all we had were platitudes...

"No, I won't believe it. There must be something, anything!" The words popped out much louder than intended. I turned to see Diana at the foot of the bed and a thought struck me.

Maybe there was something?

"Diana, what if we did for her what Lycan did for you? Could we turn her into a werewolf? It would fight whatever is happening to her now, wouldn't it?" The hope in me was an instant flare, and I clung to it in desperation.

Diana's lips pursed and she glanced at the two doctors in their lab coats. They quickly put their heads together, murmuring too low for my ears. Dominic rested a hand gently on my shoulder before he crouched in front of me. He hadn't left the room once, staying near to me, bringing me water for Bee. Bringing me food and water for myself.

"Sienna. I want very much for Bethany to be saved, both for you and for Will," He reached up and brushed tears off my cheeks that I didn't know I'd been shedding. "There is a strong chance that she will not make it. Her body can't handle this level of trauma for much longer. No human can."

I took a shaking breath, understanding clearly that he was trying his best to prepare me for another death. Preparing me to lose another friend who'd so swiftly become a part of my family.

Will let out a low moan from where he knelt on the other side of the bed, Bethany's hand clutched in his own. "My beautiful girl please do not leave me, not now. Not when I finally admitted that I love you. Please stay with me."

A gasp escaped Evangeline, but otherwise the room was

silent.

I turned at the sound of the door closing. The doctors were gone.

Had they given up?

"They've gone to get the serum to try and turn her into a werewolf. They'll hand it off to a human servant as they will be...otherwise disposed at that time but it's simple enough to administer. She just needs to drink it in the midnight hour," Diana said softly. "The process is painful, and the chance that it will kill her is high. But this is also killing her, and we have no answer for it. For good or for ill, we will try."

I gritted my teeth and nodded. "Thank you."

Diana's jaw was tight, and her eyes had a distinct feral look to them. "Do not thank me yet. For even if she lives, she may take years to forgive you the pain you are about to cause her. I...cannot stay for this. I cannot relive my own journey to the moonlight. My wolves are calling to me, I must go."

With that she turned on her heel and left the room swiftly, closing the door behind her.

The silence was heavy for a few minutes, broken by the young prince.

"It is a good idea," Will said quietly. "I would marry her still, werewolf, human, whatever she is, I would marry her. She is the best thing that could have ever happened to me. I was just too stubborn to see it."

It was about damn time he figured it out. I only hoped it was not too little, too late.

The Duchess smoothed a hand over Bethany's head, her words echoing my thoughts. "Let us hope that we are not too late for our sweet Bee."

Bethany's muttering under her breath was the only sound for the next hour, competing only with the howls from outside. Sometimes it sounded as if she were trying to sing or hum a song that only she could hear. Other times she thrashed and begged for death, her body arching up from the heels of her feet to the crown of her head. That was the worst, when we had to try and hold her down so she wouldn't hurt herself.

We kept circulating the cold cloths, setting her in an ice bath, pouring water down her throat. None of it truly helped, but it gave us something to do as we watched her wage a war only she could fight.

The Duchess paced the room, a finger tapping against her chin. "What could have happened to her? If I thought that Edmund had known that Bethany was special to you, I'd say that he'd somehow set a plague upon her before we left, but I do not see how he could have known. We were so careful. If he'd have tried to kill anyone, it would be you, Sienna."

Dominic let out a low growl. Though I didn't think the Duchess was wrong. Edmund would want me dead knowing as he did that Dominic had feelings for me. There was no way that the vampire king knew that Bethany and Will were a love match. Not even Scarlett, the traitor, had known that.

"Should we consult the books again?" Diana and Evangeline had spent hours doing that earlier but had come up empty. "The keep here has an extensive library, almost as big as the Fae. Surely, we could've missed something," Dominic asked. "Or perhaps we can consult the Oracle? She's made herself scarce. Probably in the kitchen eating."

When Dominic the sceptic was suggesting the Oracle, I knew we'd reached the end of the road. They were grasping at straws. We all were. But Will nodded anyway.

"We have time before they try the serum on her. Surely in all the archives here there must be something that can guide us. We just need to look harder."

The three of them nodded, almost in unison.

"Then we will find it," the Duchess said, striding toward the door. "Come, it will go faster with the three of us."

"You're leaving?" I stared at the three of them. Not that I was afraid to be alone with Bethany. More that if she died...I didn't want her to pass without Will at her side too.

The very thought had my throat tightening and my eyes burning once more. I clutched at Bee's hand a little tighter. She couldn't die, she just couldn't.

Dominic bent and kissed me, his lips pressing hard to mine. "Rafe and Jack are just outside the door if you need us, or if... something with Bethany changes, have them come get us. We have to try and find a cure. We have to do *something*."

I blinked and the three of them were gone, their vampiric speed on full display. Rafe poked his head in a moment later.

"Miss, we're here if you need us, just holler."

A pair of boys, barely out of their teens, guarding a door, keeping thousands of werewolves at bay.

I grimaced. "Cold comfort those two are."

Bethany moaned. "Cold comfort. You remember how

the ocean felt when we swam to the boat? Like ice. I thought I'd freeze to death."

That was the most coherent she'd been since I'd entered the room hours earlier. "Me too." I smoothed a hand over her face again. "So cold."

Her eyes popped open, a lighter blue than they'd ever been before, almost like glacier ice.

"Bee?"

"I..." she trailed off, jerked away from my touch, and stumbled to her feet. She was wearing only a thin night shift and that was only for modesty's sake. I tried to get in front of her, but she was quick.

Far quicker than she'd been the day before.

Panic clawed at my chest. "Bethany, please, you shouldn't be up."

Her eyes locked on me, and her nostrils flared. "I...want things I shouldn't, Sienna." Her throat bobbed up and down and she swallowed hard as she stared at my neck.

Without another word, she spun away from me and ran for the balcony doors, leaping through and off the ledge with the speed of a cat.

I didn't stop to think. I just tore ass after her. At the last second, I let out a holler. "Get the General! She's headed for the harbor!"

Then, I murmured a prayer and vaulted off the second-floor balcony.

The landing was better than I deserved, a hedgerow of thick shrubbery saving me from the worst of it. Still, it took me precious seconds to untangle myself and give chase. By the time I bolted after Bethany, she was almost out of sight. I did my best to close the gap, but she was lightning fast, and I was no match.

A few moments later, I caught sight of her silhouette, backlit by the brilliant white light of the full moon. She ran straight for the water and dove in without hesitation, disappearing beneath the gently lapping waves.

I hit the edge of the water a minute later, the cold of the ocean making me gasp as I followed her. My heart nearly beat out of my chest as I searched the waves for any sign of her, but there was nothing.

"Bee!" I called, the saltwater filling my throat and nostrils, stinging my eyes. I dove under the waves and searched frantically for any sign of her. I was just about to swim up for air when I saw her, cross-legged, sitting Suk asana at the bottom of the ocean.

Grabbing her by the hair I hauled her upward.

We broke the surface of the water and she gasped. Her face, for the first time, was not as red, but more of a light pink.

"That's better," she whispered.

Even so, the water around her heated quickly. The movement of the waves took the warmth away and replaced it with fresh cold. I was shivering, but Bee seemed content.

"Just let me float here," she said, her eyes still glazed and strange, but at least she wasn't moaning.

I couldn't bring myself to deny her. "Okay, but stay close to shore," I whispered, "and stay quiet."

The cold was sapping my strength and, with no sun and the brisk night winds whipping, I knew I'd be hypothermic soon if I didn't get out. I waded back to where I could touch and stood, sloshing my way out of the shallows.

What the hell was happening? They'd sworn it wasn't possible, but the speed...the longing for something forbidden...

Was she—?

I shut down the thought before it bloomed into full panic. If Bethany was doing the impossible, then it would likely kill her before her transformation was complete. Better it was an illness. At least that could be fixed. And, while it wasn't a cure, if the ocean gave her relief, then so be it.

I stood on the shore a moment and stared at her floating on her back, as if she didn't have a care in the world. Which would have been all well and good except...

A low growl rumbled behind me, the animosity in it clear as a bell.

I turned slowly, already knowing what I'd see, but hoping I was imagining things. The massive, dark red wolf had its teeth bared and its hackles up as it stalked toward me.

Relief rolled over me and I let out a nervous chuckle. "Thank the gods. Lochlin, it's me, Sienna."

The low rumbling snarls didn't ease off, not a bit.

I held out my hands to my sides, palms facing him as I turned. "Loch?"

He growled and juked to the left, driving me down the beach.

"Have you lost your fucking mind? Lochlin!" I snapped his name, and he snapped his teeth right back at me.

Diana's words echoed in my head.

"You'll all need to stay sequestered, and behind locked doors, for your own safety. We take every precaution, and try to keep it as civilized as possible, but I only have so much control once the pull of the moon takes hold. We will be outdoors, largely, but it's very unpredictable."

Well, we surely weren't inside or safe. And this Lochlin was anything but predictable right now.

"Look, my friend, I'm going to take a step back." I very clearly recalled that he couldn't swim. And while the water was fucking cold as ice, I'd take hypothermia over being mauled by Dominic's best friend.

I took a step back again, but he cut around to the side of me. And, this time, he managed to get between me and the ocean. As I stared into his snarling face, massive teeth gleaming in the moonlight, a sense of dread closed over me.

I didn't want to take over Lochlin's wolf, but there was no other choice.

Taking a deep breath, I reached for the power inside of me. Before I could do anything, though, something broke my concentration.

The steady hum of an ironwood staff.

"Step away from my mate, Lochlin."

CHAPTER 10

Dominic

The staff vibrated in my hands as I spun it between Lochlin and Sienna. I didn't dare take my eyes off him as I spoke to her.

"Sienna, get in the water."

For once she didn't argue and Lochlin didn't try to stop her, his attention firmly fixed on me now.

He bared his teeth, his black lips shaking as he growled low in his throat.

"Old friend do not make this mistake. We'll both end up hurt, but I swear you will take the worst of it." In a flash, I flitted to the water's edge, blocking Sienna and a floating Bethany from his line of sight.

Hazel eyes narrowed, and his muscles bunched a split second before he leapt at me. I spun my staff hard, driving the long edge of it across the length of his body and hurling him down the beach.

The blow seemed to barely register as he was on his

feet without so much as a how-do-you-do. I adjusted my stance again, once more putting myself between him and the girls.

"Loch, do you remember the battle of Angel Ridge? I used you like a horse; you were so much bigger than me then. We rode into the fight; we couldn't have been more than thirteen years old. I fell off twice, and you protected me. You were nearly run through, and I took a man's head to save you. It was my first true kill in battle."

The only thing that *could* potentially get through to a werewolf during the full moon was strong memories and deep bonds. I was banking on our long-standing friendship, despite our ups and downs.

He slunk toward me, slowly, his belly against the sand as he crept closer, the sound of his fur brushing through the grains, and his low rumble the only sounds I could hear.

I kept the ironwood staff spinning, moving it around me, hoping I could distract him. But he never once wavered...never once tracked the movement of the staff instead of my body.

Fuck, this was bad.

"Dom..." Sienna murmured my name as a warning.

"Quiet. I need him to focus on me," I spoke, again

keeping my eyes on him. "I have to knock him out, then we can get you two back to the keep."

And then Lochlin could go on his merry fucking way, wolfing out with his pack.

There was a split second where my attention was pulled away from him, movement on the right side of me up the beach and Lochlin took it.

He leapt forward, knocking me to the ground. I barely managed to get the staff between us, using it to hold him off me.

Sienna gasped, but he never looked at her.

His jaws snapped inches from my face as I held him back, pressing the ironwood to his throat.

"Idiot!" I yelled, not sure if I was yelling at him or myself. I knew better than to take my gaze off a werewolf during a full moon.

I was suddenly regretting the decision to demand Rafe and Jack stay behind. They were young and inexperienced. I'd already marked them as traitors and dragged them into this mess. I couldn't have their deaths on my head too.

Lochlin scrabbled at the sand to either side of my body, fighting desperately to get to me, his claws leaving long furrows in the sand. Drool slid off the edge of his mouth and landed on my neck, hot and foul.

"You smell like shit," I snapped. "Like you've been eating horse dung again."

He roared, fury etching his features, and I managed to get my feet between us, and flipped him over my head, his body twisting in mid-air to land on his feet like a cat.

The only problem with that was that it put him closer to Sienna.

She stood behind him now as he faced me, her skin pale and eyes wide, a hand to her mouth. But once more he seemed not to care that she was there, his focus was solely placed on me.

"Come on then, mutt. Let's see what you've got." I bent to a fighting stance, bringing the ironwood around my body, spinning it faster and faster.

Lochlin kicked out his back legs, spraying sand against Sienna's skirt. She didn't move.

Lochlin ran at me once more, jaw gaping wide, swiping at my legs with his front claws. I drove the staff straight down into the front of his leg, snapping the bone. I didn't stop. I had to immobilize him.

"You could have just backed off!" I swung the staff, catching him in the other leg and knocking him off his feet.

With one more swift move, I drove the staff into the side of his head.

He went limp on the sand.

I ran past him and reached for Sienna's hand. "Quickly."

"Bee!" She turned to her friend who floated still in the water. "We can't leave her!"

"They can't bother me here," she said softly, her voice carrying easily. "I'll stay deep enough."

Sienna balked, and I bent to scoop her up.

"Dominic, we cannot leave her! The werewolves can swim, it's just Lochlin that can't! You know this!"

I did know it. Lochlin sank like a stone because he was part fae and something about that mixture gave him a weakness to water. But the other werewolves were strong swimmers.

"Pull her out if you can," I turned my back on her, thinking that Lochlin would still be flat on the ground.

Luck was not a lady tonight; she was a right bitch.

Not only was Lochlin up on his feet, but he'd also been joined by two other wolves, padding close so silently that I'd not heard even the whisper of sand sliding under their massive paws.

"Stay in the water, Sienna!" I kept my eyes locked on

Lochlin, some small hope that I might be able to reach him.

"Old friend, you have to hear me. If you wake in the morning and find my blood on your mouth you will never forgive yourself." I took a step back toward the water, and he followed.

Inch by inch we moved in tandem, until my heels were right at the edge of the water.

"Loch." I said his name with all the emotion I could muster. Not because I thought he was going to die. No, I didn't want to be the one to kill him, any more than he would want to kill me. But if it came down to it, Lochlin would die before I'd let him at Sienna in this form.

"Swim out." I said.

"Already going, Bee, come on, deeper water is colder water."

The two werewolves with Lochlin twitched their ears and the one on my left, a shaggy gray furred monster, leapt in their direction.

I swung the staff, and connected with his head, the crack of bone and ironwood a resounding toll through the air. The werewolf flew sideways, taking down Lochlin and the other wolf.

It was the only moment I was going to get. I spun and dove into the water, swimming hard to reach the girls. The light of the moon reflected bright on the water's surface, tiny sparkles dancing under the water with each stroke of my arm.

"Swim, swim!" I commanded Sienna. Maybe if we could get to a boat, we'd be able to defend ourselves easier.

A set of jaws clamped down on my right foot and dragged me backward. The fear was not for me, or even for the pain.

Sienna was swimming out there, the kraken was off to Blackthorne Harbor, and she and Bethany were sitting ducks.

I was dragged bodily through the water, no matter that I thrashed and kicked at the face belonging to the teeth holding me. I didn't recognize the wolf that pulled me back onto the beach.

Dark brown, with patches of white, the wolf stood over me, teeth barred as she stared down at me. There was nothing human about the eyes, or what was behind them. Only a feral need for blood and destruction.

I hammered a fist straight up into her chest, knocking the wind out of her, cracking ribs as I flipped her off me and made it to a crouch.

Sienna screamed something from out in the water.

"No, you stay where you are!" I shouted back, getting the gist of it despite the blood rushing through my body. I did a quick count of the wolves. Thirteen now, too many even for me to survive.

The wolf I'd knocked off me finally caught her breath, but I had already decided it was time to go on the defensive. I kicked the ironwood staff I'd left behind up and into my hands, spun it once and drove the point hard into the side of her body.

I could keep them at bay, but for how long?

Long enough for the sun to rise and kill me, even as it gave them back their human shapes?

The thought of burning up like that again nearly brought me to my knees. I couldn't do it. It'd be better to die fighting.

The wolves came at me in waves, teeth and claws, driving at me from all sides. It was all I could do to keep moving, to keep pushing them back. The blows I delivered would have cracked vampire skulls, killed humans, but the wolves were made like bricks and mortar. Their bones were thicker, their ligaments and muscles tougher.

The only weakness that they had were their cubs—of which none were nearby—or the fact that when they were on two legs, they were far more easily killed.

"Why could you not be allergic to silver?" I snarled, breathless as I downed yet another wolf that I'd already dispatched twice before. I noted that Lochlin was holding back, and I realized that he'd called in the reinforcements. I'd seen him do it in battle before.

He would wait until I was on my knees, and then he would take me and deliver the killing blow.

The moon had dipped some, but we were a long way from sunrise, and the wounds I'd sustained were slowly draining me. Bites to both arms and a leg. Multiple slashes from claws across my chest, back and the back of my head.

They were slowing me down.

Lochlin paced around the pack waiting for the moment.

It came far sooner than I could have expected.

Two wolves rushed me, one from either side. I swung hard for the closer one on my right, pivoting off my toe to bring down a crushing blow to the back of the wolf's head. I stepped back and jabbed the point of the ironwood at the second wolf, driving the staff down his gullet, choking him.

With a grunt I picked him up with the staff and flung the body far out over the other werewolves.

"Are we done?" I roared the words, my own fangs descended which told me just how close I was to losing control myself.

There was a distinctive splash of water as someone left the safety of the ocean.

Distraction, a simple distraction and Lochlin was on me. His weight bore me to the sand, two other wolves helped him pin me down, but it was my best friend's teeth that sunk into my neck.

Not quite killing me.

Holding me.

Fucking wolves liked to play with their food, just like cats, during the full moon.

"Lochlin, you let him go right now!" Sienna's voice was like a whip crack through the air. "Let him go, or I swear to every god this miserable world has that I will force my will on yours."

I'd have warned her right then not to, that it wasn't possible. That there was nothing she could do when they were in this state. Hell, there was nothing I could do. I couldn't even see past the thick fur of the three werewolves holding me down.

She let out a screech, I tried to flip Lochlin off me, but then the werewolves peeled away and I could see her clearly.

Sienna's hand was wrapped around the nose of one of the werewolves, her eyes shining bright gold, as if she were glowing from within.

The wolf stared at her, transfixed, as did the others.

"Sienna, whatever you're going to do, do it," I said, my voice thick with my own blood.

She was shaking, the wolf she was hanging onto lunged at her, and then it was howling, screaming in pain.

I rolled to my knees, staring. Unable to comprehend just what I was seeing. Because it was impossible. During the light of the full moon, when the wolves were in full control of their bodies, it was impossible for them to shift back to two legs.

And yet...that was exactly what she was doing.

CHAPTER 11

Sienna

The rest of the wolves scattered from the beach like cockroaches, yipping and howling as they loped off. Loch's ginger wolf spared us one, long look before joining them.

"What's happened?" the woman lying on the beach croaked, pushing herself shakily to her feet. She shot a glance to Dominic and then back to me. "Did I...hurt someone?"

Her heart-shaped face was filled with remorse and confusion, and the adrenaline-laced fury coursing through me drained away in one fell swoop.

I shook my head slowly, shaky now, my muscles twitching and trembling. "No. No, we're all alright."

A glance at Dominic, who nodded, confirming my words.

He was okay, thank the gods, but this man was hellbent on giving me a heart attack. A bolt of guilt shot through me as I realized he didn't have a death-wish so much as he wished to protect me from harm which, no matter how hard I tried, I could not seem to avoid.

The woman before me blanched suddenly, her muscles spasming.

"You need to go," she whispered, moments before her body began to contort.

She wasn't an evil person. Her goal wasn't to do us harm, but the creature inside her couldn't curtail its nature in the face of the moon's power. She could no more control it than the scorpion could its sting. It would be cruel of me to keep forcing her or any of the rest of them back into their human forms.

We needed to get the hell back to the keep where we belonged like we'd been told from the start.

Dominic was way ahead of me and had waded into the water to collect Bee. She tried to fight him at first, but despite his injuries, he easily overpowered her, and she quieted in his arms with a groan.

"So bloody hot, damn you."

The woman before me had dropped to the ground, limbs already morphing.

"We need to make haste," Dominic said, moving to

scoop me up as well.

"My legs are cramping up. I need to use them," I said, already breaking into a jog.

He kept pace with me, sending me worried, sidelong glances as we went.

"I'm fine. I just need to get warm is all. It's Bee we need to worry about."

Because even after all this terror and mayhem, our problem was far from solved.

A look at Bee's face as she hung limply over Dom's shoulder told me that she was once again rife with fever.

How long could a body take that before simply giving up?

Could she survive this? And even if she did, would she be able to cope with her new reality?

I didn't know, but I prayed we would have the chance to find out.

We made it back to the keep without further incident, but when we stepped through the door, it was to find Will by the door tugging on his boots.

"Where the fuck were you three?" he demanded, eyes going wide as he took stock of us all.

"Bee made a run for it. She wanted to be in the water

where it's cold," I managed through numb lips as I paused to bolt the door shut. "I followed her, Dom followed me, the wolves are feeling froggy tonight, and well...you get the picture."

Will stepped in and slid Bee from Dominic's shoulders into his own arms, taking a moment to brush the wet hair from her flushed face.

"Casualties?"

"Negative," Dom replied, already turning to face me. "Hot shower, right now. I'll get cleaned up as well and we will all meet up afterward."

"Alright."

His jaw swung wide at my easy agreement, but as much as I didn't want to let Bee out of my sight, I was too cold and exhausted to argue with him.

"I'll give Bee a cold bath in my quarters. Come there when you're done. A servant dropped off the serum, and we have a couple hours until midnight," Will said with a quick nod before heading off.

"Are you okay?" Dom murmured, studying my face with concern.

I wasn't. Not really. The amount of power I'd used had left me on empty, and I was running on pure fumes at this point. In fact...

"I could use your help."

The relief on his face made me feel slightly less stupid for asking. "Come on, Starshine," he murmured as he scooped me up into his arms.

My head lolled back as he carried me up the steps to the bathroom connected to his bedroom. He sat me down at the vanity and then turned the shower on full blast. Seconds later, the room filled with steam, and I let out a groan. Dom dropped to his knees in front of me and peeled my clothes away. He didn't bother to take off his own as he lifted me up in one fell swoop, urging me to wrap my legs around his waist as he cupped my bottom.

When the hot water hit my icy skin, I couldn't contain the hiss that left my lips. If this was anything like the relief Bee felt when she'd dove into the ocean, I could see why she'd risk life and limb to do it. The soothing heat seeped into my skin, stealing away the chill. Dominic held me there, swaying to and fro, until I stopped shivering. When I felt like I could finally stand on my own, I lowered my feet, and he released me. I turned to face the steamy spray, saying a prayer of thanks. For the water. For this man. For us all surviving when we should've been dead.

Again.

Gentle hands on my scalp stole those thoughts as the scent of lavender filled my senses.

He was washing my hair. The big, bad General of the Vampire Army was washing my fucking hair, and I loved it. I let my shoulders slump, enjoying the moment. All too soon, this brief pleasure would be just a memory as the real world came crashing in again.

But for now? In this moment?

I was content.

It was only when the suds had long been washed away and the hot water grew tepid that I finally stirred.

"We should go. Bethany needs us."

Dominic nodded. "She does. Go ahead and dress. Once I change, I'll stop at the kitchens, heat you some stew and then meet you in Will's quarters."

I moved to leave the shower and then stopped short. It needed to be said.

"Thank you, Dom. For...everything."

I didn't wait for his response. I just grabbed a towel from the rack and scurried away.

By the time I reached Will's room twenty minutes later, my hair was dry, I was cocooned in a thick, plush robe and feeling something close to human. I paused and sucked in a deep breath.

Please, gods, let her be even a little bit better...

I rapped lightly on the door and stepped inside to find Will crouched over Bee, who lay prone in his massive bed, covered in only a top-sheet. Her face was beet red, and her eyes once again glassy. It was what I expected, but that didn't make it hurt any less.

"Hey," I said, leaving the door ajar for Dom and padding toward the bed. "How are you holding up?"

Will lifted his fear-ravaged face and shook his head. "I'm not. Sienna...I did this. Me. I did this to her." He turned back to lay his hand on Bee's forehead. "Her organs are going to fail under the heat soon and there is literally nothing I can do to stop it."

"We just need a little more time. At midnight, we can—"

"Stop. Just stop it," he murmured, hanging his head. "We both know she's too weak to handle a change like that right now. If she dies, it's all my fault."

As much as that was technically true, him blaming himself wasn't rational. "You couldn't have possibly known, Will. It's never happened this way before, and you are no Oracle. You have to stop with the recriminations, if only to free up your mind to think of something else we can do for Bee."

Even as I said the words, I realized that I'd been doing the same thing. Not blaming myself for Bee's condition but blaming Dom for Jordan's passing. Like Will, he had no way of predicting that Jordan would follow him into battle. And still, I'd used him as a scapegoat...a soft place to aim my anger. But sometimes terrible things happened, and they were no one's fault. It was just the way the chips fell.

I told Will as much, and again, he shook his head.

"I should've never bitten her. She would be hale and hearty right now. So fucking selfish and stupid!" He shoved himself to his feet and seemed to be about to put his fist through the stone wall when Dominic walked in with two ceramic crocks.

"She's made it this far. She'll make it a while longer. Long enough to try the serum. Hopefully the doctors and Diana will return shortly after if things go awry." Dom handed me my steaming cup, and then brought the other to his brother. "We'll come up with something. We've beaten the odds every single time, and we're all still standing. Seems silly to bet against ourselves now, doesn't it?"

Will accepted the stew with a grateful nod and took one of the chairs set up in a semi-circle around the bed. "You're right. This isn't the end. I'd know it in my soul, wouldn't I? If I was about to lose my only true love?"

I could see the hope blazing once again in his blue eyes, and I didn't have the heart to tell him. Love didn't have fuck-all to do with it. Fate was a cruel, ruthless bitch. She could give or take without warning or regret, turning a random, Sunday picnic into Armageddon without so much as a by-your-leave.

I wanted Bee to survive more than anything on this earth, but the truth was, the odds of that were shrinking with every passing, feverish second. Her pulse was pounding so fast, like a tiny kick drum in her neck thumping a staccato beat. She wasn't getting better.

For the next hour and a half, we took turns mopping Bee's brow with ice water and talking to her in low, comforting tones. As midnight loomed, though, I could feel the tension in the room ratchet up. By five of, it felt like a vice-grip threatening to choke me to death.

"So, we're agreed? We're going to try it?"

"I don't see we have a choice," Dominic said, his expression grave. "Her heart is working so hard, and her fever is still so high. If anything, she seems to be getting worse."

As much as I hated to risk it, I couldn't argue with him. "I agree." I'd regained some of my strength after getting warm and eating, so that was something, at least. "And if things go south, I will do everything in my power to heal her."

At the end of the day, that was the best I could do for her. But damn, did I wish I had some sort of guidance. Where were the dreams and soothsaying voices when you needed them?

"You've got to try."

I looked up to find Myrr the Oracle standing in the doorway, a sympathetic smile on her wizened face.

I gnawed at my lip, hesitant, and then asked the question anyway. "Is that a prophecy or...?"

"Sorry, kiddo. I wish I could say it was. I just noticed the time and thought I'd come up for moral support. If you'd rather it was just the three of you, though..."

"No," I said, confirming it was alright with a quick glance toward Will, who nodded. "The more people pulling for her, the better."

"We'd better get ready. We only have a minute or two,"

Dom said, moving closer to Bee's bedside.

Will held the vial of midnight blue liquid in front of him, turning it this way and that before handing it to me. Then, he lifted Bee into a sitting position and moved to lay behind her, supporting her head and back against his chest. My heart gave a squeeze as he leaned close and whispered something in her ear. If only she could truly hear him right now. I was sure he was murmuring the words she'd so been longing for.

The grandfather clock down the hall let out the first, hollow gong of the hour, and I sat beside Bee and held the vial to her lips.

"I love you, my dear friend," I whispered as I tipped my hand, upending the contents into her mouth.

She swallowed reflexively, I let out a shuddering breath.

We knew from what Diana had told us that it would take some time to see any reaction at all but that, once it came, it would swiftly turn to chaos. I felt so wrong, but I prayed for a long, miserable night of agony for my friend because that meant it was working.

"Sienna, you should probably stand up and take a step away from the bed, just in case she—"

Will broke off as Bethany sat up straight and let out a

snarl. In her open mouth I could see a blue ball the size of a marble, gleaming on her tongue. She spat it out onto the floor and lunged toward me, but Dominic was too quick, grabbing me and spiriting me across the room in a flash.

"Bethany, it's alright. It's me," Will said, leaping to his feet to stand over her.

"Will?" she croaked, cocking her head as she stared at him.

"Yes, love. It's Will," he crooned, reaching for her. "You're alright. I'm going to take care of you."

Bee didn't reply. She just dove headlong at his wrist, fangs gleaming in the dim light a second before they plunged into his flesh. Will let out a grunt but didn't pull away as she sucked and moaned, eyes rolling back in her head as she fed.

"Welp, looks like we have our answer now, kittens. Seems like your friend's body rejected the whole werewolf thing because she is, in fact, a vampire now," Myrr chirped from her spot tucked in the corner of the room.

She paused, spying Will's half-empty, now cold stew.

"So, now that we've got that all squared away, is this up for grabs, or...?"

CHAPTER 12

Dominic

I was determined that today would be the day.

The first in what felt like forever where Sienna wouldn't be attacked by a human, wolf, vampire, or death-worm, so help me gods.

Not that she was prioritizing that goal nearly as much as me. She hadn't even slept in my room the night before. She'd wound up setting up a cot at Bethany's bedside, which led to me sleeping on the floor beside them and Will, just in case the wolves started sniffing around. Luckily, the rest of the full moon night had passed without further incident, and we'd all awakened whole and unscathed.

Even Bethany had been looking better when the sun had risen. Diana and the team of doctors had come to check on her quickly before getting some sleep and agreed she was improving. She still wasn't fully in the clear yet. The fever was still touch and go, albeit not as high, and she'd drunk too much too fast and wound up vomiting up most of her first blood meal before taking a smaller one from Will in the wee hours. She was alive, though, and right now, that was all that mattered.

If I was a betting man, I'd have said she was going to be okay...physically, at least. What being unwittingly turned into a blood-drinking monster would do to a person's psyche, though, remained to be seen.

I yanked on my boots and headed out of my quarters, down the hall toward Diana's war room. We'd all been summoned around noon, likely so the queen could get a full report on Bethany's condition and make some decisions about the coming days in light of it. I was about to walk into the room when a raspy voice called my name.

I turned to find a haggard Lochlin standing a few feet away, his bloodshot eyes full of regret.

"Forgive me, my brother."

I tamped down my instinctive fury on Sienna's behalf, realizing with a start how much her presence in my life had begun to influence me. Old Dominic would have torn his head off. Then again, old Dominic would never have felt as protective of anyone as I did Sienna, so the point was moot. Whatever the case, my anger flickered out as quickly as it had come.

"There's nothing to forgive. You can no more help what you did than I can stop myself from drinking blood."

Loch closed his eyes in relief and then opened them, the familiar gleam back in place. "And here I was sure ye were gonna be a right prick about the whole thing and make me grovel."

My lips twitched and I shrugged. "The day is new. Plenty of time for you to fuck something up that requires groveling to fix, old friend."

"That be the truth, alright." He slapped me affectionately on the shoulder and we walked into the war room together.

"Looks like everyone is here, now," Diana said, looking up as we entered.

She was seated between Sienna and the Oracle at the massive table while Will, the Duchess, and Lycan sat across from them.

If Loch looked tired, Diana looked ten times worse.

"Everything alright?" I asked, studying the usually impenetrable woman before me. Had something else happened the night before that we didn't know about?

"Fine, yes," she said with a clipped nod. "The full moon

is draining, and I got little sleep once it waned. I couldn't stop thinking about poor Bethany. We..." she trailed off and forced a tight smile, "share a strange bond now. I remember what it felt like to turn, my body breaking down completely only to mend back together again to form something completely new. There are the obvious changes, but there is also a grieving for what you used to be and all that you've lost. I fear that we've witnessed only the beginning of her pain. But I digress. At least she will be less vulnerable now. That's a plus. She might even be able to help our cause in some way. Most of all, though, we are grateful that she is still with us, yes?"

She slapped both hands on the table and glanced around as we all nodded and chimed in our agreement.

"I haven't seen her since dawn. How is she now?"

"Still not fully lucid, but she seems much more comfortable physically. I'm hoping she'll be awake and alert enough to have a conversation by nightfall," Will said, his eyes downcast.

"And will you be the one to have that conversation with her, or...?"

"Actually, if it's alright with you all, I'd like to be the one to tell her," Sienna said.

Will shot her a puzzled look. "Why? I'm the one who did it. The least I can do is break the news to her."

"I don't want to hurt your feelings, Will, but I need to be honest. I think it's best if she has some time to come to terms with things...alone."

He winced and nodded in understanding. "And by alone you really just mean without me there."

It was clear that Sienna realized she'd hit a nerve, but to her credit, she didn't waiver.

"For now, yes. She won't be herself. Hell, she won't even know who *herself* is anymore. She might react impulsively; say things she doesn't mean..." Her golden gaze collided with mine and I realized she was speaking of herself as much as she was Bethany. "She's got enough to grapple with right now without adding a bunch of guilt and apologies to the pile."

I hated to see my brother so low, but Sienna was right, and he knew it.

"Can you at least tell her that I love her and am ready to talk whenever she is. All she need do is summon me?"

"I can, and I will."

"Excellent," Diana said. "That taken care of, what else did I miss last night? Do we have an update on the

Hunters? Any sense of them, Sienna?"

"Nothing," Sienna replied, pursing her lips. "Obviously, we were pretty busy, but I did try to reach out this morning. They are still too far away to establish contact."

"That's good news, to say the least. I imagine they're enjoying their freedom. In the interim, though, let's assume that they are moving ever closer and get back into preparation mode," Diana said. "Full steam ahead on weapon's prep and training."

"I'll be running two separate sparring sessions this afternoon with some of the less seasoned warriors," Lycan said, his arm resting protectively around my aunt's shoulders. I raised my eyebrows at that but said nothing. Evangeline fairly purred under his touch.

"I've committed to spending some time with the two girls I brought here. I think the full moon stuff was a bit triggering for them. They were under lock and key and unharmed, but with Edmund's hunt fresh on their minds, I'm sure it was a long night." The Duchess shifted her attention to Sienna. "Then, if possible, I'd love to see Bethany. She needs to hear the news from her best friend, but only her own kind can truly understand what it is to be a vampire. It might help for her to have an unbiased ear to bend about what she's feeling and experiencing."

It was Sienna's turn to wince, but she too, took the words in stride. "Understood. I left her sleeping with Rafe guarding the door. I gave him instructions to send word for me as soon as she awakens. Until then, I'm going to do some training myself."

"I'll join you," I said with a nod.

The others got their marching orders from Diana, and we filed out a few minutes later.

"Are you feeling strong enough to do this?" I asked Sienna as we broke off and made our way to the courtyard. There was a whole covered section, and the weather was once again mild. Hopefully, the fresh air would do us both some good and clear our heads.

"Am I feeling strong enough?" she asked with a snort, poking a thumb at her chest. "The question is, are you feeling strong enough, big guy. Because I'm feeling awfully froggy today. In fact, I'm feeling so amped right now, I might even be able to take a General down."

"Ah, Starshine, you know if you want me to go down all you need to do is ask." Maybe the playful banter was just bravado after another horror of a night, but I went with it because that was clearly what she needed at the moment.

She laughed and rolled her eyes as expected. "Leave it to you to make it sexual."

"Don't leave the door wide open and then act surprised when I walk through it," I teased, resisting the urge to give her pert bottom a pat as she jogged lightly down the stone steps into the courtyard.

"Enough flirting with me, General. Choose your weapon."

She waved a hand to the wall lined with every manner of sparring weapon, from dulled broadswords to wooden battleaxes.

"Let me guess...the ironwood staff?" she asked, a wary look in her eyes.

"That would be wholly unfair and we're already a piss-poor match for sparring. How about I pick for you, and you pick for me?" I said with a shrug. "What could be more sporting than that?"

She squinted suspiciously, but then nodded. "Alright, then I choose the dagger for you," she said, pointing to a tiny, dulled blade all the way at the end of the row.

I went and retrieved it with a smirk. The thing was so small, it was nearly hidden in my hand. "Very tricky, m'lady. But I will warn you, I've done my fair share of training with something similar for those occasions where all a soldier has left is his wits and a wimpy little dagger tucked in his boot." I shook my head with mock regret. "You've gravely underestimated me."

"We'll see," she replied, cocking her head in a haughty way that told me she was getting into the spirit.

Gods bless her stubborn heart, my woman couldn't bring herself to back down from a challenge, no matter how daunting. After a long and difficult few days, blowing off some steam would be good for her, regardless of the outcome.

"And for me?" she asked, arching a brow.

I surveyed the options and finally selected one.

"A whip, hmm?" she asked, a curious gleam in her eye. "Mind if I ask why?"

"Without training, it's basically useless," I replied with a shrug. "But you're a quick study, and if I give you a few pointers before we start, you should be able t—"

The sound of a *crack* interrupted my thoughts, and I drew back in surprise as a clump of grass shot from the ground, inches from my feet.

I looked up to find Sienna watching me, a saucy smile spreading across her full lips.

"When I used to dance, I played at being a dominatrix. Better tips and all."

She reeled off a series of dizzying moves, making the whip skim through the air as she twisted and turned. Graceful as a ballerina, deadly as a viper.

When she stopped, she was a foot away from me and the whip was wrapped around my waist like a belt.

"It seems as if you have gravely underestimated me as well, General."

"Well, fuck me, then," I marveled, a rusty laugh breaking free of my chest even as my loins tightened. Gods, she was sexy.

And brave.

And funny.

And everything I'd ever wanted in a mate but didn't know it.

Which meant we needed to win this war if I wanted a lifetime with her.

"Caught you," she whispered, rolling up on her toes and planting a kiss on my lips.

I kissed her back and then pressed the dagger harder against her kidney, so she could feel it.

"Aye, but the price was steep."

Her eyes widened, and I took advantage of her surprise, spinning away and freeing myself from the whip.

We faced off like opponents in the ring and she began to circle me, her whip in constant motion.

"What are the rules here?" she asked, on high alert now that she knew the game was truly afoot. "Are we allowed to use everything in our arsenal? Super speed? Super strength?" Her eyes drifted to my mouth. "Fangs?"

I shrugged. "We'll be fighting vampires, albeit most not as strong as me. Still makes the most sense if you know what that entails so you can prepare. If you're armed with a reinforced whip as well as a dragon blood tree stake, you can deliver a killing blow. I think swinging a sword hard enough to separate a vampire from its head would be much more difficult. This will be excellent training for you."

I scanned the wall and snagged a stake made of balsa wood—safer for practice—and tossed it to her.

"Let's go."

Again, she began to circle me, the whip writhing, flickering against the ground like a tongue.

I did what any vampire would do in my shoes and went for speed and power, crossing the distance between us in one massive lunge. Her eyes went wide as the dull blade pressed against her neck.

"Okay, now that was really fast," she breathed.

I could see the pulse flickering in her throat, and it took all I had not to scrape the very tips of my fangs against it. Her pupils dilated, and she slid her free hand between us, cupped my already aching cock. Blood pounded in my ears as she gave it a long, firm, squeeze.

A moment later, the dagger was flying from my hands, across the courtyard, and her stake was at my chest.

I shook my head, a wry smile curling my lips. "Well done, Starshine."

"Doubt it will work in battle, but there is value in knowing your opponent," she replied with a cheeky wink.

For the next hour, we sparred. I was tentative at first, but it was almost as if she'd grown stronger the more she explored her power. She was also skilled with the whip and thought on her feet. Soon enough, I actually had to work at besting her.

That was good.

But was it good enough?

The thought of her fighting another male—one who wasn't me, with a much sharper knife who made full use of his fangs and strength—made my stomach churn.

She stood across from me and I let the brakes off, bull-rushing her with everything I had. Her whip was fast, but not fast enough to stop me as I took her to the ground in a tangled heap.

I lay above her, heart in my throat as I stared down at the face I would burn cities for.

"Please don't do this to me," I muttered. "Stay at the ready for healing, but do not try to fight in this war. If I lost you, I might as well be dead myself."

Her fierce gaze went soft as she reached up and traced my jaw with her fingertip.

"You know I have no choice."

I leaned forward and pressed my forehead to hers. That's when I heard them.

The birds.

They came in like an army of silent assassins, the only sound the beating of their massive wings. So many wings.

I rolled to my side and lurched to my feet, dagger in hand, but paused at the spectacle. Dozens...no, hundreds of raptors filled the courtyard. Eagles, buzzards, falcons and hawks. They were everywhere and suddenly they were swarming me. Talons, beaks and wings battered my body.

The damage they inflicted was minimal, but the chaos alone and the knowledge of what *could* have been had Sienna commanded it was chilling.

Before I could even fathom and game plan, they were gone, taking to the skies once again.

"Pretty good, right?"

I turned to find Sienna standing a few feet away, brows lifted in question.

"Pretty good," I agreed with a nod.

The display did make me feel slightly better. She was infinitely more powerful than the average human, and her potential was even greater. I just knew that the time to test it all was in the heat of battle.

But my musings were wasted. Sienna was going to do exactly what she wanted to do, and no one—not even me—was going to stop her. The best I could do was to give her the best possible chance of survival.

I turned and met her gaze as I gripped my dagger with grim determination.

"Again."

CHAPTER 13

Sienna

The pull of the bowstring made my right arm tremble as I pinched it between my thumb and fingers. Aiming down the line of targets, I let out a breath and loosed the arrow. Before I even saw if it landed, I had my second arrow up, aimed at a target to the left.

"Keep breathing, keep shooting." Dominic stood just behind me, a hand to my lower back. "I can feel you holding your breath again."

I aimed and loosed the second arrow, sweat trickling down the side of my face, scooped up the third arrow and took a gulping breath as I focused on the third target, the furthest to the left.

As soon as I loosed the arrow, praying I hit the bullseye, I lowered my bow, my numb fingers nearly dropping it.

"Not bad at all," Lycan's voice called out over the training grounds. Dominic flexed his fingers gently against my lower back as we turned to face Lycan and...Evangeline with the two girls she'd rescued. I remembered them both well. Aubrey, who had nearly bested me in archery as Will's partner, and Anya. The latter had been a bit of a snake, doing whatever it took to progress in the games, even if it meant stabbing someone else—like me—in the back.

Aubrey bit her lower lip. "I thought we were the only ones who made it out?"

Of course, they wouldn't have given a single shit about me missing ahead of them. They likely hadn't even noticed.

"Well, one must take opportunities where they are offered if you want to survive this world." Dominic spoke before I could gather my thoughts. And then he bent and kissed me, long enough to make his claim obvious. I smiled, my heart doing stupid funny flopping motions in my chest.

He grinned and pulled back. "Lycan, will you walk with me? I would discuss the usage of some of your weaponry."

"Of course, General." Lycan tipped his head and then turned and kissed Evangeline so thoroughly I found myself blushing and looking away, as if I were seeing something far too private for public consumption.

Dominic grunted as if he'd been sacked. "I thought Will

was shitting me when he'd said he'd walked in on you two. Apparently, I owe my brother a hundred gold coins now."

Lycan laughed as he left with a still head shaking Dominic, their male banter one made of a long-standing working relationship perhaps?

"Well." Evangeline's dark cheeks were flushed as she cleared her throat and faced me. "Have you spoken with Bethany yet?"

Anya gasped. "The maid? The maid is here too? How, when so many of the Harvest girls were killed?"

I looked at Anya, really looked at her. I had hoped that her brush with death and the trauma of the trip would've made her less awful "She arrived with me. We escaped together."

Her eyes were defiant. "What makes you two so special? I know why the Duchess saved the two of us."

Evangeline turned to face her charges, and I found myself taking a step back.

"I saved you because you were the ones I could get to in time. No more, no less," the Duchess began, her voice trembling with anger. I found myself not really listening to the rest as she tore a strip off the two girls. I was too preoccupied as the flutter of wings and the brush of a mind against my own had me turning away from them.

A moment later, a large black crow swept toward me, flying hard, as if it were being pursued. But there was nothing behind it. I held up my hand, offering the bird my wrist and he—no, she—dive bombed to land. I closed my eyes as her talons wrapped carefully around my forearm, lifted my other hand, and set it on her back.

Images from the bird flickered to me in rapid succession.

The Hunters were on the move, but still at their own pace. At this rate, we had a few days, less if they picked up speed. There were a dozen of them, they weren't even attacking as much as they could be. Currently they were lounging at a series of hot springs, feasting on local wildlife before they were ready to move on.

"Good job," I whispered. "Be safe my feathered friend."

The crow didn't lift off but bent her head and pressed it to the side of my face.

Another image. This one not from the crow, but from another female.

One of the Hunters.

I swallowed hard as her thoughts came through so clear, it was almost like I was hearing the kraken again.

We fear him, the one with the crown. He will destroy us if we don't obey, but we wish only to be left alone.

If you would stop us, you need to find a way to stop him.

We saw you in the clearing. We felt your connection to Spirit. Felt that you would hear us.

The male. Jyx. He is the one that the vampire King controls.

My stomach lurched with excitement. This was more information than I could have possibly hoped for.

I tried to formulate the right questions. "*Thank you. I don't know if I can stop him. Can you tell me how?*"

Break the connection. The male with the red eyes must be killed if we are to be free.

The connection between myself and the female hunter shattered suddenly. She roared in pain and there was a flash of teeth, a brilliant burst of red eyes and the presence of a male pressing in on my mind.

Once my hunger for flight and flesh is slaked, I will destroy you all.

I steeled my shoulders and stood up a little straighter. He would have to go through me first.

I don't know what made me think to do it, but I reached through the connection and used my power like a strike, as if I'd literally reached him and cuffed him across the head.

The connection between us broke, but not before I saw him fall away from the female, releasing her limp form.

I dropped to my knees, my hand still pressing on the crow's back as she clutched my forearm. She ruffled her feathers and let out a soft clucking noise, butting her head against mine repeatedly until I loosened my hold and released her.

She flew away, and I stayed there on the hard packed gravel, the blood rushing through me, adrenaline pumping wildly. I swallowed hard and looked up to see only Evangeline left on the training grounds with me.

"What happened? What did the crow bring you for news?" Her voice held that same sharpness that said she meant business.

Dominic and Lycan were jogging back toward us. I didn't think they'd have gone far, not with all that had happened to both Evangeline and me of late.

"Let's find Diana and the others. It pertains to...everyone." I wobbled up to my feet and found myself scooping up the bow and two arrows from the ground. I probably didn't need the weapon but, in that moment, it gave me a sense of control. I was a decent shot. I could defend myself at a distance.

Dominic reached me, but not before the Duchess.

Evangeline made her way to me and slid her arm through mine. "You should get cleaned up first. You stink."

Another time it would have made me laugh. As it was, my mind and heart knew it was no time for prettying up.

Dominic didn't say a word, but his eyes spoke loud and clear. He had my back in the most literal of senses. His palm spread wide across my lower back once more, his touch steadying me. I gave him a smile.

"No, we go straight to Diana."

She snorted—most unlike her—and we hurried up the slope away from the training grounds.

Lycan moved to Evangeline's other side, silent as Dominic, letting Evangeline and I speak.

We had a few minutes before we would reach Diana and I took advantage of it. "I thought Anya and Aubrey would have been a little more..."

"Grateful? Humble? Less stupid?" Evangeline sighed. "I saved them because they were the only ones I could get to as the others set out to hunt the girls. Now they feel like they were special *because* I saved them." She shook her head and her arm tightened on mine. "Every life is precious; I cannot believe they would—"

"Treat me like shit still?" I did smile then, though it was bitter. "Some people never change, Evangeline. Like Edmund."

Dominic grunted his agreement, but otherwise kept his thoughts to himself.

The Duchess nodded slowly. "I should have taken you up on your offer Lycan, all those years ago. We'd have been better off with Edmund dead. But at the time...I thought he'd have time to change. To grow. All he did was grow into a larger monster."

Lycan swept her hand up to his mouth and kissed the back of it, his gaze solidly on her. "There is no room for recriminations now, love. You saved Diana. That will have to be enough."

I cleared my throat and spoke. "Where did the girls go, anyway? Back to their rooms?"

She gave me a sidelong look. "I sent them to the kitchens. To wash dishes and mop floors to gain some perspective. I would have preferred to let them continue to rest, but I will not tolerate that kind of behavior. Ungrateful brats."

I couldn't deny that I liked the sound of the two women who'd been cruel to me sent to do menial work. And in reality, the kitchen was probably one of the safest places for them.

The door to the war room was closed tight. I knocked against it with the tip of my bow.

"Enter."

The four of us let ourselves into the room. She glanced up, and must've seen something in my face, because she stiffened instantly.

"What is it?"

"The Hunters are still moving slowly, but that's going to change. The big male, with the red eyes is being controlled by Edmund." I didn't waste time with my words. Bethany needed me, and I'd been away from her long enough now.

Diana looked us over. "So, the plan has not changed then, not truly. We need to kill Edmund and the Hunters."

I shook my head. "The Hunters do not want a fight. The female said they wish only to be left alone. Then she was attacked by the male that Edmund is controlling." I looked at Dominic then. "How is he controlling the male?"

Jyx.

The male's name was Jyx.

"I'm betting there is a collar on the male that connects to a cuff that the King wears," Dominic said, frowning. "It hasn't been used in a long time, though. We didn't utilize the Hunters during the skirmishes after the Veil fell, so it has to be close to a hundred years old."

"Meaning?" Diana said. "What exactly?"

"That we don't know how effective it is," Dominic said. "Edmund has never used the collar before, and things have changed since the fall of the Veil. Bottom line is that Edmund might have complete control, or he might only have partial control. I'm guessing the latter, or they'd have already been here. I know the male Sienna is talking about. He's a brute of the highest order and has killed two other males in the past when they tried to take his spot as the alpha of the group."

I drew a breath, knowing that this conversation was about to go long.

"I...if you don't need me further, I would like to go see Bethany."

Diana gave me a wave. "Give her my best."

Dominic made a move as if to follow me. I shook my head. "Stay and help figure out our next steps. I'll see you later."

Later.

As in later in the room we had agreed to start sharing.

A flush curled up my neck as I turned and hurried away,

toward Will's room where Bee had been sleeping.

I reached the door, still holding the bow and arrows. I knocked and Bee's voice called out.

"Come in."

I stepped through the doorway to see her sitting up, a huge number of pillows stuffed all around her as if she couldn't sit on her own. Her cheeks were still rather pink, but the rest of her face was a creamy white, her eyes brighter than I'd ever seen them.

"Sienna! Oh, I'm so glad you're here! I'm starving and everyone is just telling me that I have to wait for you. Why in the world would they say that? Are you my maid now?" She laughed and patted the spot next to her.

I glanced at the thermos sitting on the table. Quite sure I knew what was in it. I laid down the bow and arrow and spoke as I walked toward the table. "Well, I guess because they wanted me to talk to you about...how things have changed. How you've changed since the bite that Will—"

"Oh, I already know! I'm a vampire now!"

I turned, thermos in hand to see Bee grinning at me, fucking beaming. With wee tiny fangs peeking out past her lips.

I stared at her, stunned. "You aren't upset with him?"

"Upset with him? Now I can be with him, Sienna! I mean...if he still wants me?" She suddenly looked worried. "Maybe he only liked me because I was weak?"

"Jesus, he better not turn you down now," I muttered as I unscrewed the thermos and poured a cup of still steaming blood out into the lid. I swallowed down the bile rising in my throat as I handed it to Bee.

She took a sip and moaned before she tipped it back like she was taking a shot. "Oh, that is so good! I mean, I know I should be grossed out and all, but honestly it tastes like...like heaven."

I sat on the edge of the bed. "Maybe let it settle a bit before you have more. You didn't do well that first round."

She grimaced. "I forgot about that! It feels like it was so long ago...I was so hungry though, and I just...I couldn't help myself."

I looked at my friend, truly looked at her. "You aren't freaked out at all? Mad? Scared?"

She shook her head. "This is like...a dream. A good dream. This is the only way I'd have ever been able to be with Will. Truly be with him. It was an impossible thing, and yet it happened. I could never be mad, or even scared."

Bethany glanced at the thermos, and I saw her hands

twitch. I poured her another cup and gave it to her. She sipped it down, slower this time.

"That's good," I said, because I wasn't sure what else to say. I had prepared myself to tell her to calm down, to take it one day at a time, that she'd get used to drinking blood. But she didn't need me for any of that. "Um. Do you want to see Will? He's pretty shook about this being his fault."

Her eyes widened. "He thinks I'll be mad at him, doesn't he?"

I nodded. "He thinks you won't ever talk to him again. That you won't love him now. And seeing as he loves you, that's a bit of a blow, as you can imagine."

Her jaw dropped. "He truly loves me, then?"

"From his lips to my ears, he said it out loud." I smiled at her, and she squealed and jumped out of bed, nearly toppling over.

"I've got to go find him!"

I barely managed to grab her arm; she was so damn fast. "You stay here. You've got to get your strength up. I'll...I'll go find him."

I left her in the room, sucking back the last of the thermos as I went to find Will. As happy as I was for her, I couldn't help this tiny feeling that rooted in the bottom of my heart. That she got to be with Will, that they could be a true couple, that she wouldn't grow old and die in his arms while he lived on and on.

Which left me wondering...

Just how the fuck were Dominic and I going to make it?

CHAPTER 14
Dominic

I watched Sienna go, striding off toward Bethany's room, seeing the strength in her. We'd been sparring for hours, into the evening. She'd also used her power to talk to both a crow and a Hunter apparently, and now she was off to feed a brand-new vampire as if this was just one of her daily duties.

Of course, she didn't know that I'd instructed Rafe and Jack to stay close to Will's chambers to keep an eye on both women. Sienna was as safe as she was going to be here in the keep while I was busy dealing with other matters.

Like the current conversation...

"This collar and cuff," Diana said, eyeing me shrewdly. "We don't have any records on it."

"You wouldn't." I pulled my attention back to her table and the map spread out over the entirety of it. "We have kept the secret of how the Hunters are controlled very close. Only the king, and the general of the army are privy to the details of how they are kept on a tight enough leash to actually use them in battle."

Diana tapped her fingers along the edge of the map. "So when we kill Edmund, what then? Do the Hunters become wilder yet? We would have to kill them all. I am loathe to do it as they are as much a part of this world as we are..."

I stared at my half-sister. "You'd spare them?"

She shrugged. "If the kraken can be tamed, then why not the Hunters? The question is, how many of us will die before we kill Edmund?"

"I think," Lycan said softly, "that we will be dependent on Sienna to reach the Hunters. That she's already made contact with one of them, that in itself is a bloody miracle. But if she can continue to connect with them, perhaps once Edmund loses his control, they will turn to her for guidance. It will save lives. *She* will save lives."

My jaw ticked as I stared at the map and all the lines on it. The direction so many were already being sent. The exodus had begun, sending women and children, those too old and too young to fight, away to safety. Malach had reluctantly agreed to allow Diana's people onto his lands.

Though it had cost her...

She owed the winged bastard a favor and no one—myself included—was comfortable with the open-ended 'owing a favor' shit when it came to the Fallen. They were sneaky fuckers at best, and downright deadly at worst, with a combination of speed and power that made me grateful there were not many of them left.

"Sienna is not a warrior," I said, coming back to the moment at hand.

"Perhaps not like you and I," Diana countered. "But that does not mean she shouldn't be there, or that she can't fight. Her power is like nothing we've ever seen. And we need her there."

"I'll second that!" Myrr bellowed from behind a curtain at the window.

Everyone in the room jumped, and I couldn't help the snarl on my lips. I noted that Lycan had shoved Evangeline behind him.

"What the fuck, Myrr?" Diana snapped. "You were welcomed to the meeting as always but—"

"Ah well, none of you even looked for spies! Nor did one of you smell me. But I am quite sure that there will be food brought here soon...For the guests that are arriving." She grinned, though it looked more like a grimace to me.

"Food, correct? Please tell me not all the cooks have left!"

"What guests?" I moved swiftly to the window where she stood, shoving her out of the way.

At a full speed gallop, a contingent raced toward the keep. I narrowed my eyes, recognizing the man in the front.

"Open the gates!" I called as I headed out of the room.

Diana trailed behind as we made our way through the keep to the covered courtyard.

Her long, easy stride matched mine and again I was struck at the similarities between us. My sister was strong, and wise and I felt an unexpected wash of pride that she was a part of my family.

The main gates were slowly being opened, just enough that a single horse and rider could make it through at a time. Wider with each second, then two riders at a time, and finally the entire contingent flashed through.

"There he is, the bastard son!" Raven called.

"Raven, what are you doing here?" I stared at my old friend. "I thought you'd head back to Seattle?"

"I brought him."

I turned to see Nicholas of Southwind dismount. "Edmund sent men after us. We lost four on the way. Raven was in as much danger as us, being your friend and known ally from past wars."

"And my mother? She is safe in Italy?"

Nicholas inclined his head. "She is."

I let out a sigh of relief as Diana stepped toward Nicholas and held out a hand. "You've done well. But why are you here? The last message we had was that you would hit Edmund from behind, while we kept his attention on the front of the fight."

Nicholas gave a quick nod, his face tight with anger.

"Edmund is killing anyone that has ever even hinted that they might be for William. I brought all the fighters and lordlings I could with me. The rest that sided with him...they aren't going to change their minds. He's controlling them with fear."

I looked at the men, a little less than fifty. Fifty men out of hundreds. Fifty that were willing to stand with Will. That could not be.

"There are no others that see Will as the King?" I couldn't keep the shock out of my voice. I could not believe that so many would stand with Edmund.

Nicholas's face tightened, his dark eyes glittering with anger. "There were, I would say more than double what we have here, with us at first. Scarlett turned them. Said that you would have wanted her to stand with the rightful king. That the worm had your brain, and that Will was in love with a human. That you needed to be put out of your misery like a broken-legged horse, same for Will." He spat to the side. "She's awfully good at twisting a story, General."

Bile rose to my throat at the thought of her.

How could I have been so blind?

Diana nodded. "It is no surprise. That we even have fifty more men is excellent. Peter," she called to one of the werewolves standing guard, "see the men to quarters below. Get them food and get their animals settled as well. Nicholas, please come with us. We were just discussing the battle site. We will have to adjust now that things have changed."

Nicholas paled a little, but he nodded and fell into step behind Diana.

Raven did the same with me. "That was a bloody ride I would not like to have again."

I glanced at him. "No? You don't like running for your life straight into enemy territory?"

He laughed, his smile flashing wide as he winked at more than one of the women we passed. "Not my idea of a good time. Now, where is she?"

I blinked at him. "Are you serious?"

"I rode all this way to see the vixen that stole your heart, would you deny me?" Raven gave me a look that said he was not going to give up on this. Even though I knew it was a front for the real reason that he was here. He was a strong fighter, and I would be glad to have him at my side.

"I have a meeting, Raven. And as a battle-hardened vampire, we could use your insight."

"Shh. I don't like people remembering that." He tapped a finger to his mouth just as Sienna and Bethany stepped out of a side hall.

Sienna's fiery red hair caught the light, and she fairly sparkled, like a flame come to life. But Raven's eyes went past her to Bethany. Her blonde hair and blue eyes were pale, and exactly the current fashion of vampire beauty. He went to one knee, and I rolled my eyes. But damn, the man had style, I'd give him that.

"She doth teach the torches to burn bright! It seems she hangs upon the cheek of night." He managed to catch Bethany's hand and bring it to his lips, clearly not recalling he'd met Bethany in the past, albeit when she was a maid...and human.

"Oh!" Bethany was obviously caught off guard but too polite to pull away. Sienna frowned, and it was then I saw the bow and arrow in her hand. She had it raised in a flash, the arrow tip pressed to Raven's neck.

"No one invited your touch," Sienna snapped.

Raven rolled his eyes to her, and his grin was wider yet. "Gods. You would pick a fierce tigress to bed. Tell me, Dom, has she clawed your back apart yet? I'll admit, I prefer a softer touch from my woman." He pressed his lips again to Bethany's hand and Sienna jabbed him hard enough in the neck to roll him away from her friend.

"As you can see, Raven, Sienna does not need me to fight her battles." But I would be there regardless, doing all I could to keep her safe.

I changed the subject swiftly, not liking the direction of my thoughts. "Where is Will?"

"Being stupid," Bethany snapped as she bent and helped Raven to his feet.

My eyebrows shot up. "Stupid?"

"He seems to think he doesn't deserve Bee," Sienna said, her aim still floating toward Raven. Raven, who was currently pulling Bethany closer yet to his side.

Well, if there was one thing that would pull Will's head

out of his ass, it was a little competition.

"Raven, perhaps you would like Bethany to show you around the keep?" I said.

Raven gave a bow over Bethany's hand. "It would be my greatest pleasure if the lady would accompany me?"

"I'd love to," Bethany said, and they turned together, walking back the way Sienna and Bee had come.

"Should I shoot you now or later?" Sienna hissed. "Why would you do that?"

"Will needs a kick to the balls. Raven will not force her to do anything she doesn't want to. And if I let slip that...Rafe..." I beckoned to my soldier that was lurking in the shadows. "If you would be so kind as to let slip to my brother that Raven is currently entertaining Lady Bethany?"

Rafe smiled, just a flash as he saluted me and then was gone just as quick.

"Oh, that is devious, I like it." Sienna finally lowered her bow and arrow. "We were headed to the library. I'd still like to go and look for something."

The tone in her voice said she had a very specific thing she wanted to look for. One that she was not about to share with me.

Before I could even offer to escort her, she went on tip toe, kissed me quickly and then left me standing there in the hall.

I made my way to Diana's war room once more.

"Where is William?" Diana asked, her voice sharp.

"I'm sure he will be here soon," I said as I made my way around the room. Lochlin had joined us now, and I placed myself at his side. The taste of Sienna's mouth still on mine, I let myself imagine, just for a moment, if we could have a life together. But it ended...the same as every other time I imagined us together. With her growing old and dying in my arms. Frail. Human. So very mortal.

"What will happen to her, after all this is over?" Lochlin asked me quietly, snapping me out of my thoughts.

I knew who he meant. There was only one woman whose life was uncertain through all this, one woman who had no true place in our world despite the power she showed.

"I don't truly know. I don't want to even think about her leaving, even if we could give her a pass that she would remain unmolested on the mainland." I frowned, my heart squeezing uncomfortably.

Terribly.

"She can't stay here forever, mate," Lochlin said softly. "Even with a clan backing her, she is marked by so many that she just doesn't fit. Not safely. We already know there are those that would harm her."

He was not wrong. She had a connection to vampires and werewolves, and the stories of her controlling the werewolf and the kraken were flying through the ranks.

"I don't want to think about her leaving, not yet." My voice was hoarse. "I want her to be happy, and safe, even if it means I'm cutting my own heart out to make it happen for her."

Lycan gave a grunt and stepped closer to us. "I met my heart mate hundreds of years ago." His eyes drifted to Evangeline. "I had a mate, had children, did my duty, but my heart lay elsewhere. There was nothing that could be done about it." He shrugged. "And other than a fever dream that I seem to be living in now, I know that it won't last. Because the world dinna give us that option. So be glad of the time you have, then let her go and live a life away from you, safe. That's my advice, lad. Live while you can, for tomorrow, we face the darkness. One that none of us may come back from."

CHAPTER 15

Sienna

The soft sound of snoring that woke me the next morning probably should've irritated me, but instead, I smiled to myself. If someone told me a few months ago that I'd be charmed by the sound of a vampire male snoring beside me, I'd have thought they were nuts. Then again, Dominic wasn't just a vampire male. He was *my* male, and each moment I got to spend with him was precious.

He let out a grunt and rolled to his side, slinging an arm around my hips. Still sleeping, he let out a little growl and flexed against me, letting me feel his hard length pressing against my thigh.

Something hot stirred inside me, but I tamped it down with a sigh. If I wanted more nights like last and more mornings like this, however fleeting the fates made them be, I needed to get my ass in gear.

I made quick, quiet work of getting ready and left the

room with one last glance at the bed. He didn't require nearly as much sleep as I did, but last night had been a particularly late one for him. He, Raven, Nicholas, and Will had stayed in Diana's war room deep into the night, discussing strategies along with Lycan, the Duchess and Loch long after I'd gone to the Queen's study... And long after I'd headed straight to Dominic's quarters rather than back to the war room because I needed time alone to process what I'd learned.

The smile faded from my lips as I closed the door softly and made my way down the hall.

Don't fall down that dark, depressing rabbit-hole. You have work to do.

I rounded the corner and headed toward the quarters I'd shared with Bee. When I stepped inside, I found her already awake and donning a pair of boots.

"I was wondering if I'd find you here, or if you were in Will's room..."

She let out an indelicate snort. "Not quite. He's so busy feasting on shame and guilt for something he didn't even mean to do, I don't think he sees me at all right now. Which, I really wish he did, because I look amazing. Get a load of this skin, Sienna," she continued, beaming as she rushed to the full-length mirror in the corner of the room. "No annoying little spots, or blemishes. No tiny, fine line between my eyes reminding me that I frown too much. I look like I just spent a month at a spa in Paris or somewhere fancy like that, don't I?"

"Amazing what ingesting pints of someone else's blood could do for a girl," I almost replied. Instead, I swallowed the acidic response. She didn't deserve that. Despite Will's current mental state, he'd come around and soon, they'd be together. Forever, assuming they survived the coming war.

Because they were both immortal now.

An ache spread across my chest, but I managed a smile.

"You look beautiful, Bee. But you always were."

She rolled her eyes and wheeled around to face me. "Exactly what a friend would say. And still, even my tush looks perkier."

I forced myself to admire her bottom with as much enthusiasm as I could muster, but it was a relief when she finally pulled her attention from the mirror.

"The Duchess made sure I...ate this morning, and I'm brimming with energy, almost like I'm touching a live wire or something. Do you think we could go down and do some training together? I know I probably won't be ready soon enough to be of any real help, but maybe..."

Her cornflower eyes were full of hope, and I wasn't about to shoot her down by telling her how far behind the curve she was. I needed to practice anyway, and there was no harm in taking her with me.

"Okay, just remember to stick close to me and don't go near the sun. We've got to stay in the covered part of the courtyard." This got me a second eyeroll, and I held up a hand. "It's not second-nature to you yet, and I worry, that's all. Sue me for caring."

Her gaze went soft, and she came closer to give my shoulder a squeeze. "I appreciate you so much, Sienna. And I really appreciate all you did for me at the harbor. Thank gods you weren't injured. I only remember bits and pieces, but I know I put you in danger, and I'm so sorry for that."

"No need for all that. We're ride or die, me and you," I reminded her, pulling away to make for the door. Usually, I hated mushy conversations like this because they made me uncomfortable. Right now, though, hot on the heels of Jordan's death and facing the very real possibility of losing more friends, her words were making me weepy.

And weepy bitches didn't win wars.

"Let's do some sparring."

An hour later, I was flat on my ass for what felt like the millionth time and secretly praying for death.

"Whoohoo, this is fun!" Bee shouted, sharing a high five with Lochlin, who couldn't help but grin in response to her unadulterated joy.

I'd be joyful too if I could toss a hundred-and-forty-pound woman clear across the courtyard. For fuck's sake, she didn't even have to bend at the knees to do it, I marveled, rubbing the aching small of my back. I was holding my own compared to what a normal human could withstand, but unlike Dom, Bee gave no quarter when it came to using her sheer power and it was kicking my ass.

"Shoot, Sienna. Did I hurt you?" she asked, appearing at my side a nanosecond later. "I really don't know my own strength yet, and then I get so excited, I forget that you—" She broke off and cleared her throat, looking at a spot over my shoulder somewhere. "Um, I forget that not everyone is a vampire."

I pushed myself to stand with a wince.

She's your best living friend. Do not sic the birds on her. Do not sic—

"Amazing," Dominic called from the archway leading from the keep to the courtyard. He shook his head in awe. "If I didn't see it with my own eyes, I wouldn't believe it, Bethany."

He moved to my side and planted a firm kiss on my mouth. "Morning, love."

I barely got out a mumbled hello before his attention was firmly back on Bee.

"No more fever, no more pain?" Dominic asked.

"All gone," she confirmed, chuckling. "I woke up super hungry again, but other than that, I feel good. The coolest part is that stuff that should hurt doesn't. Well, most things. Lochlin changed into his wolf form a little while ago, and knocked me ass over tea kettle, and I felt it."

"We definitely don't feel pain to the level that humans do," he said, nodding. "But I'll warn you, when it hurts, it *hurts*."

I could tell by his wince that he was thinking back to the day when he'd nearly been burned to death by the sun. I still didn't know which of us was more traumatized by the event, me, Dom, or Will.

But after nearly a week of catastrophes and wondering if I was about to lose someone else I cared for, everyone was alright. Will was rid of the bloodworm, Bee seemed to be handling her transition just fine, and Dominic's burns were healed.

I should be ecstatic.

And the larger part of me was. But the other, shitty, selfish part was jealous as hell, and I couldn't just turn it off like a faucet.

"I'm going to head inside and get some lunch," I said, apparently to myself. Loch and Dominic were busy showing Bee how to hold a battle-axe the size of Thor's fucking hammer and didn't even glance my way. "Okey dokey...and while I'm at it, I'm going to drink some bleach and maybe stick my finger in a light socket."

Still nothing.

Perfect.

"Whatever." I walked away, grumbling as I made futile attempts to stretch out my sore lower back. "Oh, Bethany, you're so strong and fast. Oooh, Bethany, I can't believe how quick you're catching on!"

My sneering mouth puckered into an "o" of surprise as I walked directly into a brick wall.

Dominic.

Dominic was the wall.

"What happened?" I asked, lifting my brows. "Did Bee's head get so big listening to you fawn all over her that she floated into the atmosphere, and you need my bow skills to shoot her down, or something else?"

Dom's lips twitched and I realized he was awfully close to laughing. Annoying tears stung my eyes as I tried to shove him aside.

"Glad one of us is amused at the fact that even if we make it to the other side of this nightmare, we are on borrowed time."

It wasn't fair, but hey, neither was life.

The twinkle in Dom's eye faded, replaced by a fierce light as he cupped my chin. "Amused? Ah, Starshine, if you only knew. Aside from how to protect you, it's all I think about. It's like my soul is being wrenched in two."

"And here I thought that vampires didn't have a soul," I managed dully.

"I assure you; we do. And mine is forever tied to yours. But that is a problem for another day. For now, if you are set on joining this fight, I need to focus on making sure you get through it whole. That's my only goal right now."

I blinked at him as a realization settled over me.

He wasn't spending his time training Bee instead of me because he liked her more or suddenly had some silly crush. He was doing it so she could better protect me.

"It's wrong, I know," he whispered, dipping his head to trace my lips with his fingertips. "I do care about her as a friend and even as a potential sister-in-law one day. But the truth of it is, Sienna...the thing that matters most to me in this world is you."

"I'll not have you using her like some sort of guard dog, Dominic. She's my friend." Somehow, in the midst of my pity party of one, I'd forgotten that for a moment.

"I'm aware. But I also know that the better those of us around you prepare, the better our chances of succeeding."

And of you, the fragile one of the group, surviving.

He didn't need to say it. I knew what he meant.

And I fucking hated it.

"I really am hungry, so I'm going to get some food," I said, forcing a smile. "Keep working with Bee. She's got a real knack for the hand-to-hand combat."

I left him and headed for the kitchens, feeling like the jerkiest of jerks.

The second I walked through the door, the smell of

frying bacon tickled my nose.

Nothing like a good, old fashioned 'eating my feelings' session. I wondered idly if Bee would still be capable of such a thing and then pushed the thought aside.

"Hello there, missy. We just served Her Majesty and the Oracle, so everything is still piping hot. Can I make you a plate? Eggs, bacon, sausage, biscuits, pancakes, French toast, potatoes, quiche, fruit...?"

"Yes, please."

"Which?"

"All of it. Except the fruit. Don't be shy, either. Just pile it on there."

The cook blinked at me and adjusted her white hat. "Aye, then."

A minute later, she handed me a heaping plate. I inhaled the steam pouring off it and let out a sigh.

Sometimes being human wasn't so bad.

I headed out of the kitchen and into the dining hall, where Diana, Evangeline, and Myrr sat alone at the massive table. If my plate was full, Myrr's looked like a game of Jenga. One wrong move and the whole thing would come tumbling down.

When I walked in, she was grinning as she poured what

looked like a liter of maple syrup over the whole lot.

"Sienna. Come. Sit with us," Diana said with a wan smile before taking a long pull from her coffee mug.

She'd clearly stayed up as late as Dominic, working on battle strategies, and currently looked as if the weight of the world rested on her shoulders.

Which it sort of did.

Our shoulders, at least.

I did as I was told and took a seat. For a few minutes, I ate in silence, plugging fork-loads of pancake and sausage into my mouth. It was only when I'd plowed through half my plate that my throat went tight, and I had to work to swallow.

"What is it, child?" the Duchess asked, her tone gentle.

I blinked my suddenly blurry eyes and set down my fork. "I was trying to look up some stuff about Hunters and I got sidetracked. I know it's silly but—" I cleared my throat and straightened. "I guess when I realized that Will had turned Bee into a vampire, I started to hope that maybe..."

Evangeline's gaze went soft with pity even as Myrr cut in.

"I could've told you that's not possible," she chirped, her appetite clearly unaffected as she grabbed a biscuit in one gnarled hand and a boiled egg in the other.

Diana let out a sigh. "I can't say for sure if it's the case with vampires because, according to everything we knew, Bee shouldn't have been able to become one either. But I do have to concur with Myrr. It's not widely known but healers can't be changed. Back when it was forbidden to inter-mate, there was a love match between a male wolf and a fae female who was a healer. She wanted to become one of us, and I did my best to accommodate her, to no avail. Three times, over the course of a summer, we tried. Each attempt failed. Our doctors theorized that some evolutionary force was stopping it. Healers are at the top of the food chain, so to speak. There is no more powerful being, despite what the bloodsuckers might think." She shot the Duchess a glance. "No offense."

"None taken," Evangeline replied with a sniff that let all three of us know that there was a *little* taken.

"In any case, Bethany's transformation doesn't change your circumstance, Sienna," Diana added. "You are not only a healer of the highest order, unlike anything we've ever encountered, you also possess the ability to connect with animals. That makes you the rarest of gems. An evolutionary miracle. And it has been our experience that mother nature will fight back if we try to mess with that."

I couldn't be turned into a vampire *or* a werewolf, apparently. The latter was yet another blow. Somewhere, in the back of my mind, it had been the final Hail Mary. If I wanted to be with Dominic forever, there was a way...

And that was gone now.

"I know it's hard to hear, but better now than down the line, when it's too late to change course."

I almost laughed out loud. That ship had long since set sail, and there was no turning back. I was head over heels in love with the General, and apparently, our story was still destined to end in despair.

For both of us.

"Were you planning to eat the rest of that bacon?" Myrr asked, eyeing me hopefully.

"Nope," I said, sliding the plate across the table as the Duchess leaned forward, studying my face.

"I, more than anyone, understand wanting something I thought could never be," Evangeline said with a sad smile. "But that doesn't mean you should give up hope. I never did, and there were days it was all I had to hold onto. And now look at me."

I chewed my lower lip, considering her words.

She'd suffered for over a century without Lycan before they'd been free to love. Who knew what could happen for me and Dominic? Maybe we'd get our miracle too.

"Just make sure that you embrace who you are, child. Lean into it. Recognize that you're exactly what and who you need to be. No werewolf or vampire could do what you're being called upon to do. Once you've embraced that, the rest will fall into place. I truly believe that."

I held the thought close to my heart as I opened my mouth to reply, but again, Myrr cut in. This time, though, the voice that came from her mouth was a pleasing, male baritone.

"Your enemy is but a puppet whose master lurks in darkness. I will do what I can to guide you, but the path is bathed in shadow and mystery. All I can see clearly is that your presence is integral to winning this battle. In this, you are the key, Corumbra."

The scent of lavender swamped my senses and a feeling of calm settled over me.

"What is the other voice? The one that calls to me in my dreams...the one that came from the bloodworm?"

Myrr's eyes rolled to the back of her head as the voice continued, more softly now, almost a whisper. "That's the puppet-master in the darkness trying to confuse you."

"And what about the other keys?" I demanded, a sense of panic trickling through me as the scent of lavender began to fade. "When will they come to help?"

"In time, Corumbra. In time..."

Myrr's chin dropped to her chest as the Duchess, Diana and I let out a collective breath.

"Well, that was interesting," the Queen said, her brows raised. "It felt...good. Either I'm a real sucker with terrible instincts, or that's the voice we can trust. Thoughts, Evangeline?"

The Duchess shrugged her elegant shoulders and nodded. "I agree. There was a very soothing air about it. If it is trickery, it's trickery at its very finest."

"It's no trick," I said, feeling sure of something for the first time in the longest. "Whoever that...being is, it is the voice of good. I know it in my gut."

Which meant I was right. I needed to be on the front lines of the battle to come. And Dominic?

Well, he was going to have to learn to live with it.

CHAPTER 16

Dominic

I stood in the corner of the great room like a specter as the alphas and betas of what seemed like a hundred clans poured in. Some I recognized from the previous assembly, a few others from my youth. Most, though, were strangers to me. Those I studied the closest.

There wouldn't be another attempt on Sienna's life by some crazed purist or addled wolf gone rogue. Not on my watch.

I turned my attention toward the rows of chairs that had been set out and stopped at the front row. Jordan's clan, the Killian's, were already seated. I'd expected Kavan and his next in command, but I was surprised to see his sister there as well. Elka was her name. I remembered her from the funeral. She'd taken the loss of the boy hard, and, judging by the grim set of her jaw and the feral look in her eye, vengeance was at the forefront of her mind.

I understood. My own thoughts drifted to Scarlett the

Betrayer and rage as hot as the sun filled my belly. She had stabbed me in the back and twisted the knife while she was at it. But worse? She'd killed my mate's friend, sending Sienna into a spiral of grief that I'd feared might be the end of her.

And she would pay for her treachery with her life.

I watched as Sienna approached the Killian clan, stopping first in front of Kavan and laying her hand over the crest pinned to her chest. She bent low to murmur in his ear. He embraced her and the others in the clan followed suit.

A rumble rolled through my chest, but I kept it in check. As much as I wanted her to be all mine, I knew better. She was so many things to so many people, I would have to share her in some ways.

But gods did I fucking hate it.

"Bloody hell, man. If you don't get that hangdog look off your face, they're going to think you're one of them. You've got it that bad, eh?"

I turned to see Raven standing beside me, his gaze pinned on Sienna.

"If I pay you in gold, will you shut the fuck up?"

"For all I know, I'll be dead before the week is over. I'm

going to take the laughs where I find them. And right now, you and young William are the entertainment to be sure."

I spared a glance at my brother and winced. He looked every bit as miserable as I felt. He sat slumped in the corner, staring at Bethany, who was aggressively ignoring him as she chatted away with Nicholas.

"He cornered me this morning and threatened my life, you know," Raven continued, his tone entirely unconcerned for someone who'd been on the receiving end of such a threat from the future king. "Told me to leave the maid alone or he would...how did he put it again? Ah yes, 'sever my balls and feed them to me' if I laid a finger on her. He didn't say anything about *in* her, though..." he added with a wink.

"I'd find my entertainment elsewhere from now on. Bethany is far too smart for the likes of you," I said with a feigned yawn. "One day, maybe you'll grow up and fall in love. I hope I'm alive to witness it."

He shuddered and held up a hand. "Gods, man. Do you hate me so much to curse me thusly? It will never happen." A servant passed by, and Raven went after him in hot pursuit, calling over his shoulder. "I'm going to see if I can't get a pint in this place. Talk later."

I was glad to be rid of him. Under normal circumstances he was an amusing nuisance. During these dark days, while I was glad for his support, reading the room was not his forte. Or maybe it was, and he just didn't give a shit. Either way, I was glad to see the back side of him.

"Please, everyone, take your seats. We'd like to begin now."

Diana stood at the front of the room with seven chairs lined up facing the crowd. She caught my eyes and jerked her chin, indicating for me to join her. I scanned the room one last time, taking note of the faces in the crowd. Taking a shot at Sienna here and now would be suicide, but that wasn't out of the question if madness was in play. I'd just have to stay on guard.

I strode to the front of the room just as the rest of our contingent did the same. Diana sat in the middle while Sienna, Bethany, Lycan, the Duchess, Will, and I flanked her.

Loch, Nicholas, and Raven stood against the wall as the rest of the wolves took their seats.

"Today, we plot to end Edmund the Vile's reign of tyranny. Those of you here have already pledged your swords to the cause, and for that, I thank you."

Her voice rang out, silencing all others. The respect she commanded never failed to impress me. I knew from experience it was something you earned, and she'd clearly put in the work.

"We know now that the Hunters are soon to cross our border and that Edmund plans to follow shortly behind. Initially, I considered allowing that, and taking the time to set traps and take advantage of our knowledge of the terrain. After careful consideration, I've decided that isn't an option. We need to take this war to Edmund."

Protests rolled through the room until Diana stopped them.

"Silence until I've said my piece."

It wasn't a request.

"I cannot risk our innocents, which is what we'll be doing if we allow Edmund and his dozen Hunters onto our land. They can raze an entire farm in minutes, tearing half a dozen weaker wolves apart in the process. It is not a price I'm willing to pay. I realize we were defeated last time we fought in the Vampire Territory. We had faulty intelligence and we were betrayed. This time, though, there is no inside man or woman. We rely only on ourselves."

"And the vamps you've invited to join us," a voice grumbled.

"This is true," Diana said with a grim nod. "We have become allies for the greater good. I know it's difficult to trust those who have been the enemy for centuries, but at times we must accept that there are some things bigger than ourselves. I'm going to share something with you now in hopes that it will help you understand. Lochlin?"

She inclined her head at the ginger giant, who pressed the remote in his hand.

A screen came down from the ceiling against the wall to our right, and the lights dimmed. Moments later, a presentation starting with a montage of images flickered to life. Some were paintings of Diana herself as a child hiking through the forest or swimming in the sea. For a second, I was completely sidetracked. How had I not noticed our resemblance and more so her resemblance to our father?

"These pictures are from when I was a child, and while they are paintings, they are true depictions," she said as the images shifted to others that were strictly landscape images. Stunning sunrises, sunsets, waterfalls, and beaches. A gully so blue, it almost hurt to look at it, brimming with life. I hadn't seen much of the Territory since I'd been here, but I had a feeling that things had changed.

"This next set of photos was taken yesterday."

The next slide was another group of pictures, and they sucked the air out of the room.

A grove of black, weeping willows, drooping and rotting in places. That same gully, a rancid green, thick with algae. A spit of beach barely visible beneath the white bellies of dead fish covering it.

"My family...our home is dying. It's happened slowly enough that we've grown accustomed and unseeing, but our demise is moving ever closer. We need to restore the Veil, and until Edmund is defeated, our goal cannot be met." Diana stood and gazed out at the wolves seated before her. "So, today, I am not asking for your fealty alone. I am asking for your heart. Your soul. Your very blood. We must leave it all on the battlefield, whatever it takes. Because without that, we are doomed."

For a long while—long enough that my palms began to itch—the room was silent. And then the howling began. First, one, and then a chorus that became a cacophony. It was like Jordan's funeral all over again.

Sienna must've felt it too, because she pressed her knee

against mine.

Kavan stood as the howls ceased. "We are at your service, my Queen. To the death, if need be."

She mustered an appreciative smile and sucked in a breath. "Then we proceed. Day after tomorrow, we head to the North Fort. On the way, we expect we will meet Edmund's Hunters. We have all seen or heard tales of Sienna's power. I can assure you that they've been underestimated if anything. I believe we can gain control of the Hunters and turn them against Edmund. At worst, we can neutralize them. Malach has offered a handful of his men to monitor the skies and assist if need be. It behooves the Fallen to stop the Hunters before they pass through our lands to theirs. Once we have dealt with the Hunters, we move forward to the North Tower, where we will meet and clash with Edmund and his men."

She scanned the room and then smiled.

"I don't know about you, but if I'm placing bets on who wins in a hand-to-hand battle, us or the bloodsuckers? Well...my money is on us. What say you?"

The floor all but shook with stomping as the wolves whooped and hollered in agreement.

For the next hour, Diana delegated, detailed, and

glad-handed. I had to admit, I was impressed, and very thankful I would never be king of anything. By the time it was over, I was almost convinced we had a good shot of winning this war.

Almost.

"She's amazing, isn't she?" the Duchess murmured in my ear as I stood and watched the wolves make their way to the door, still buzzing with excitement and bloodlust.

"She is that."

"I am so pleased I was right to give her to Lycan. She's a credit to our family, even if no one ever knows it."

Sienna sidled up beside me and slipped her arm through mine.

"Can you have our group stay behind for a few more minutes? I just want to talk about...what happened earlier."

The Duchess nodded and went to speak to the others as I turned to Sienna.

"Is everything alright?"

I knew she was upset when she'd left the training grounds earlier, but she'd seemed okay once I'd spoken to her.

"It's just...the Oracle spoke at lunchtime, and I thought

I should share what she said."

My stomach twisted in a knot, but I nodded anyway. "Of course."

When all the wolves had left and the seven of us were alone again, Sienna took point, pacing in front of us as she spoke.

"I know there was some question as to whether I would be most useful staying back to help heal the wounded or by joining the fight. I can now confirm that it's no longer a debate." She held my gaze. "A voice came through Myrr...one that all of us agreed was a deity or a vessel for good, at the very least. My presence on the battlefield is necessary if we are to prevail. And prevail we will."

Bethany nodded slowly, accepting these words without question, while Will stayed silent.

I, on the other hand—

"Stop with this nonsense. One day, Sienna dreams that, unless she leaves, we are all doomed. Then, the bloodworm tells her the same. Now the crone tells her she has to not only stay but join the fight." I let out a growl of frustration. "Correct me if I'm wrong but relying on a bunch of hocus pocus seems foolhardy at this point. Surely, there is mischief at play somewhere here. Who is to say what is true and what is not?" I demanded.

"I'm sorry, nephew, but I was there and heard it with my own ears," the Duchess said, leaning on Lycan for support, moral or otherwise, as she rose. "I know you want her to be safe. I want that too. But without Sienna, we are all dead. Her included. There is no escape from Edmund's wrath if we challenge him and lose."

The others all murmured their agreement, but I barely heard it as I drove my fist into the stone wall behind me.

That damned Oracle was a thorn in my side from the start. To date, she'd told us almost nothing that would be of any help. In fact, she'd seemed hellbent on putting Sienna in as much danger as possible. And now she was doing it again.

Which made her my nemesis.

"Move it, Goliath," the crone in question muttered as she scuttled past me toward the kitchen. "You should come with your own zip code, for gods' sake.

I nearly laughed at the gallows humor of it all. I'd taken on every manner of beast, from werewolves to demons, and here I was, laid low by a tiny woman older than dirt itself.

Fucking hell.

CHAPTER 17

Sienna

The day waned on after the meeting, and I was left to my own devices for the most part. Dominic was still angry that I'd demanded that I be at the battle. Not even demanded. Stated.

I didn't feel like dealing with his anger, not right then. Which meant I found myself once more taking the path to the stables. Not that I thought I'd be able to *actually* go for a ride with Havoc, I wasn't that big of a fool.

The fragile, breakable human was not going to be allowed to do anything that wasn't overseen by someone else. At this rate, I was going to have to fight Dominic to get myself to the battlefield.

Stopping in the kitchen, I snagged an apple and tucked it into my pocket. Seeing as we wouldn't be going for a ride, the least I could do was bring her a peace offering.

I frowned as I opened the door to the stable, hating that I was the weak link here. That I was the one everyone was worried about, even if they were going to let me go. I forced myself to let out a low breath and tried to push all the rough, tangled emotions with it.

Shockingly, my efforts at calming my turmoil didn't work.

"I hate this," I muttered to myself.

A few horses peered out at me as I walked the length of the barn, but I kept moving.

Havoc was at the far end, as usual. Mostly so if someone who wasn't familiar with the horse didn't think she was worth losing a limb when they tried to pet her.

I gave a low whistle, and she popped her head over her stall, her ears initially pinned back, but as soon as she saw me, they swung forward, and she gave a soft nicker.

"Hello, my beauty," I murmured as I reached her, and ran a hand down her face, sliding my fingers under her chin and scratching her gently.

Scrounging around the barn, I found a box of brushes, then let myself into her stall, shutting the door tight behind me. Havoc nuzzled at my hands, looking for the treats I normally brought.

"Okay, okay, you're right. I have something." I pulled the apple out of my pocket, and she crunched it in half, juice running from her mouth and over my fingers. I set the last half of the apple down on the ground and picked up the first brush.

I thought that perhaps by coming here, I could find the escape for my mind, but the methodical, familiar movement of grooming a horse did nothing but free my mind to wander.

The 'what if' game began to play in a loop through my head. "What if we all survive this war, Havoc? What then?" I ran a comb through the tangles of her mane, carefully pulling the knots free. "Do I just stay here and wait to die? Or should I leave, try to have a...life...without him?"

Just saying the words, they stuck in my throat, nearly gagging me. There was a terrible truth budding in my heart.

There would be no one else for me. If I left the Alpha Territories, and left Dominic behind, I couldn't see myself falling in love with anyone else. The very thought of another man touching me, of another man kissing me, was abhorrent to the point that I had to stop brushing Havoc so I could lean against the wall.

Nausea rolled so hard through me that I had to breathe slowly with my head down to calm my wild imagination.

"I'm not there yet. Hell, I might get lucky and die on the battlefield, right? Maybe during some heroic gesture that will leave me a legend to tell tales about?" I pushed off the wall and went back to brushing her, slowly, taking my time. I mean, it wasn't like training me more was going to change things at this point. We were so close to the battle now...

Havoc wrapped her head around my waist and tugged me to her chest, a soft nicker escaping her. I wrapped my arms around her neck and buried my face against her soft coat as the tears began. I didn't want to let anyone else see this crack in me, because despite my physical fragility, everyone was looking at me to be the turning point in the battle.

The healer.

The powerhouse.

The one that everyone believed would be able to help heal the Veil.

The weight of what was needed of me, not just wanted, but truly *needed* was crushing me, bit by bit. Slowly, I slid down to the straw and Havoc followed, folding her legs carefully so that she didn't step on me. I curled up in the crook of her front legs, her head and neck still holding me gently.

I was shaking, silent sobs escaping me as the tears poured down my face.

I couldn't fail my family, not again. I cried harder as that truth hit me square between the eyes. I'd failed Jordan, and I loved Bee and Dominic, Will, Lochlin, and Evangeline as if they had truly become kin to me.

Biting my lower lip, I kept my crying silent, but I couldn't stem the tears. I just had to get this out of my system, that's what I kept thinking. I had to let the pain go, but as I knelt there, the pain only increased to levels of grief that I just couldn't comprehend.

It was as if my world was being blown apart, as if everything and everyone I loved was being destroyed right in front of me and there was nothing I could do about it.

It was all I could do to keep breathing and not die right there.

Havoc whinnied softly and I gripped her mane, trying desperately to ground myself, because I began to realize that it wasn't *just* my own grief and pain I was feeling.

The horror and sorrow rampaging through me belonged to someone else.

Some*thing* else.

I closed my eyes and searched inward, following the connection to the pain. It strung out, flying away from me at high speed. The terrain flickered in the front of my mind, trees, a river, a Tower Fort, and then I was *in* the head of something else.

A Hunter. The female again.

The pain was excruciating, but it had nothing to do with the physical body and everything to do with the heart and soul that thrummed with agony.

Edmund stood in front of her, the armband that controlled the main Hunter visible as he held a massive egg up over his head. It was emerald green, with flecks of gold splattered across the shell, glinting in the light.

"You haven't been obeying...the lot of you," he spat in fury. "Don't you realize? I OWN YOU!"

I watched in horror as Edmund hurled the beautiful, precious egg against a protruding rock.

"No!"

The bellow that ripped from my throat matched that of the female Hunter. It was *her* egg. One of only two she'd ever been able to produce. Ice trickled down the back of my neck as the twisted, underdeveloped body of a tiny hunter slid across the rock, wet and steaming in the air, its head moving once, mouth open, wings fluttering and hope burned hot in my chest.

A girl.

The hatchling was a girl by the markings across her wings. Her mother's thoughts were mine, and I knew, even though I shouldn't have.

Maybe she would be okay. She would be the first in so many years, she would bring new life to the Hunters...hope for the future.

Edmund moved in a flash, far too quickly for its mother to stop him. Before she could move, his sword was falling before there could be any more wondering of the hatchling's survival.

"I think not," he growled.

The tip of his blade pierced the body of the pup, pinning it to the ground. It flopped weakly and then was still.

The blow struck me with an almost physical force, a feeling of electricity pinning me to the spot, my body frozen by what could not be.

My baby, not my baby!

The pain was next, and it was as if someone had cut my chest open and torn my heart free, yet somehow, I was still alive.

I was still alive, but I did not want to be.

The sensation of being in the barn with Havoc and also being in a forest watching my child die bounced me back and forth, and I struggled to breathe through the agony and confusion. Underneath it all, though, a growing fury burned a hole through the grief, bringing a clarity of mind nothing else could have.

An anger so hot it would rival the sun should it be allowed to run free.

The female lunged without thought to her own welfare and I snarled, lurching against Havoc's upper body as if I could help the Hunter, reaching for Edmund as I could see him in my mind. As if I could strangle him myself with my bare hands.

Kill him. I screamed the words in my mind. "KILL HIM!"

The Hunter lunged, knowing she would die, but it would be over. And just maybe her second egg would be safe, guarded by her sister. It would be worth it. The war would be over before it began. The Hunters would be free of the monster.

As her jaws shot toward the filth that had killed her child, she saw him smirk, saw him raise his hand with the cuff on it.

Jyx, the male Hunter, slammed into her body and sent her flying, crashing through a dozen trees, the splinters of wood piercing her wings in several places. That pain was nothing though, nothing.

She landed and turned to fight her way back to the monster. She would tear him in half. Destroy him.

Jyx pinned her to the ground, his jaws around her neck, squeezing the life out of her. His thoughts battered against her head, and so they battered against mine.

Submit or die.

"I would rather die than submit to you!" I screamed the words for her, and the strength of my connection to the female Hunter pushed him back a little.

As I separated my emotions from hers, I realized that this had to stop. As much as I wanted Edmund dead—and gods, I did—the two of them were too powerful for her. She would die here fighting, and we needed her still.

I swallowed, breathing heavy as the female struggled against the big male.

"We can take them, but not here. Not now. You must calm. I promise you; we will kill them both."

The female Hunter turned her mind to me, and I let her

in, let her in to see that her pain had touched me. That I felt it as if it were my own, as if it were my child that had been killed by Edmund.

Swear it that this monster will die.

"We will kill him, or die trying," I said.

Her mind brushed more deeply against mine. Did she see that I was telling her the truth? She pulled back and the last I saw was her bowing her head to the big male.

Like an elastic band being snapped I was shot fully back into my body.

Sucking wind hard, I stayed where I was, just letting my mind and body reconnect. That was terrifying and...the pain...I touched a hand to my aching heart.

The hatchling had been so small, so helpless and Edmund had just run her through. I covered my face with my hands and cried again, this time for all that was lost already...for all that we would never get back.

I don't know how long I stayed there, I only know that it was well past dark, and the air had cooled considerably. No one had come looking for me at least. I wasn't sure I wanted anyone to see me like this—a complete and utter mess of emotions.

Pushing slowly to my feet, I kissed Havoc on the nose

and let myself out of the stall.

Movement at the end of the stable startled me.

"Lass," Lochlin said, his voice careful. "Are you alright?"

I grimaced and wiped my hands over my cheeks. "How much did you hear?"

"Likely all of it. I followed you in here, keeping an eye on you. I didn't want to break your connection, but I could nah' leave you alone. Will came to check on you too, but left when he saw I was here. Said something about feeling your pain? I'm sorry I intruded." His eyes were kind as he took me in. "Come on, let's take you back to Dom."

I nodded and walked to his side, feeling weaker than ever.

"You want to tell me what happened? Who were you trying to kill?"

I shook my head, not really sure how to explain what I'd seen and have him understand why it hurt. To them, another Hunter dead was a good thing.

I couldn't unsee the hatchling struggle against Edmund's sword. Couldn't not feel that pain as if the sword had pierced me.

"The Hunters haven't been as easily controlled as he'd hoped so Edmund is using leverage now, so they all obey."

I paused and thought about where they'd been. "He's reconnected with them at the North Tower. Time's up. If we are to meet them there, we will have to do so tomorrow."

Lochlin jerked to a stop in surprise. "I'll go tell Diana." We were in the keep now, "You go to Dominic."

He didn't have to tell me twice. It was time to say all that I had to say, for after tomorrow, there might not be another chance. I picked up my pace, and all but ran to Dominic's room.

Our room.

One last night, and I wasn't going to miss my chance here. I burst through the door and Dominic spun, an ironwood staff in his hands. As soon as his eyes landed on my face, he dropped the staff. "What's wrong?"

"Edmund and the Hunters are close. Tomorrow. We need to face them tomorrow."

And without another word, I ran across the room and threw myself into his arms, my mouth finding his.

If this was to be our last night together, I didn't want a single regret, not one moment where I would say 'if only I had'...

"I love you, Dominic, General of the Vampire Army. My

captor." I pulled back and stared up at him. "Till the day I die, whenever that is, I love you with all my heart."

CHAPTER 18

Dominic

I stared down into Sienna's golden eyes, marveling at her words, feeling them all the way through my body and heart. I smoothed my hands over her tear-stained cheeks. "You aren't going to die, love. We'll find a way. Of all the people I know, you would be the one strong enough to make the change, like my sister."

"No," she whispered. "I can't. Diana, Evangeline, and Myrr, they all said the same thing. I cannot become anything other than what I am right now."

The shock of what Sienna was saying stilled my body, as if I were facing a predator. I felt it to my bones, a blow that I couldn't defend against. Her inevitable death, long before my own.

Sienna stared up at me, golden eyes wide and full of unshed tears, her fingers holding my face lightly. "Dom? I thought you knew?"

"I just thought," I shook my head, breaking the spell that

her words had cast, "I believed we'd figure it out. That we'd have more time."

More time. Like a prayer from my lips, that's all I wanted with her. More time.

Her eyes fluttered closed, and a smile drifted over her lips. "We could both die tomorrow. That would solve the problem, wouldn't it?"

I ran my hands over her face, mesmerized by the soft feel of her skin under my fingers. "You're right, we could die tomorrow. That is battle."

"So this needs to be everything, tonight," she whispered as her hands went to her own clothes. "I don't want any regrets."

Nor did I.

I swept her up by the waist and she wrapped her legs around me and held tight as she pressed soft kisses along my jawline.

"I love you, I love you, I love you," she murmured between each kiss, like a mantra.

When I reached the bed, I sat her at the very edge and dropped to my knees. With her enthusiastic help, I made quick work of her clothes, not stopping until she was naked. For a long while, I just looked at her bathed in moonlight, committing every curve, every dip and hollow, to memory. Her breath hitched under the weight of my gaze as her lips parted and she let her thighs fall open.

It was an invitation I couldn't refuse.

I gripped her hips and laid my mouth on her, groaning like I'd been in the desert for a hundred days and finally found water.

She slipped her hands into my hair as I flicked my tongue against her clit.

"Dominic," she whispered, her fingers already tightening. "Gods, that feels good."

I couldn't reply. I was too consumed with the taste of her. I drew the sensitive little pearl into my mouth and sucked gently as I batted it with my tongue. Her thighs clamped around my face tight as she flexed against me. And when I slipped a finger between her folds and began to slide it in and out, mimicking what I would do later...what I wanted to do now with my aching cock, her thighs squeezed even tighter.

Through the blaze of need, I couldn't help to think, even if I suffocated here and now, I would die happy.

"Dom, stop!" she whispered, slightly frantic.

But even as she spoke the words, her hips moved fast, her

breathing quickened.

"I want to come with you inside me."

I wanted that too, but I had every intention of having my mate and eating her too. I plunged my finger deeper into that wet heat, moved my tongue faster.

"Dom, if you don't stop, I'm going to—oh!"

Blood rushed from my head to my cock as I held her tight against my mouth. She tugged at my hair, her back bowing, her head tossing.

"Fuck!"

Feeling it all, hearing it all, was more than enough as she came in a hot, wet rush. I had to close my eyes, because if I watched, I would be done for myself.

When the storm finally passed and she stilled, I slid my finger from her and laid my head down, letting her cradle it with her thighs.

"You aren't a very good listener," she managed, her breath coming in gasps.

"The irony is thick with this one," I shot back with a low chuckle.

"Touché."

I could hear the smile in her voice, and I lifted my head to see it.

The second we locked eyes, though, it faded. "Come up here."

If anyone had told me I'd have been laid low by the expression on a woman's face, I'd have laughed. But here and now, with Sienna, the joke was on me. Her gaze was filled with so much love. So much hunger and yearning, that I'd have stolen the stars from the sky for her if she'd asked.

I stood and stripped off my clothes until I was as naked as she was.

"You're beautiful," she said, leaning forward to trace my stomach and the line of muscle leading to my thighs.

I was going to tell her the same when she dipped her head low and sucked the tip of my cock into her mouth.

"Bloody hell," I snarled, tipping my head back as her hot tongue swirled. "Sienna," I warned softly as she began to take to the job in earnest, sucking in long, deep pulls. "You said it yourself. Me inside you."

It took every ounce of self-discipline I had to pull away. "Slide back."

She skittered back along the bed until her head was on my pillow and I climbed up to join her, my knee between her thighs.

I took one nipple in my mouth and sucked as she reached between us and guided my cock home. First the head, and then the rest. Inch by agonizing inch. Her body stretched to accommodate me like a silken glove, and it was all I could do to hold still.

"Love me, Dominic," she murmured, lifting her hips to mine, bouncing gently. The drag and pull of her tight heat was pure torture, and I growled her name as I moved with her. Slowly at first, and then faster. Deeper. I pressed my face to her neck and breathed in her scent, letting it wash over me. But it was the feel of her wild pulse under my tongue that had my fangs popping free.

This was Sienna. And as much as I wanted to, I could not ask her to—

"Bite me."

Her hissed command had my whole body tensing, but she didn't stop moving those hips, her pussy working my cock over and over, getting tighter and tighter as her own release grew close.

"Do it. I need to know what it feels like. Please, Dominic," she whispered, her breath going choppy as I started to move again, pounding deeper.

"You're sure?" I managed, my throat suddenly so

parched it felt like I'd swallowed acid.

"So sure."

I couldn't help it then if I'd wanted to. The vampire in me had been invited in, and I could not deny her.

In one swift motion, I sank my fangs into her neck. The sensation alone as my teeth broke through her delicate skin and into her flesh was almost enough to make me come. But the taste of her blood sent me over the edge. It pulsed into my mouth in a hot, heady rush, slipping down my throat like a magical elixir. My balls went tight as I exploded, jerking and bucking, burying myself to the hilt.

"Oh my gods, Dominic!"

She screamed my name as I drew long and hard, fucking her, drinking her, owning her as she owned me. Her pussy clamped around me, holding me in place as it squeezed and contracted around me, over and over.

The blood rushed in my ears, and I tried to keep my sanity. Tried to brand this moment into my mind so I could call on it forever.

She shuddered beneath me, her body going soft, her arms falling to her sides.

With a heavy sigh of regret, I released her neck, licking

the puncture marks gently as I did.

I rolled to my side and dragged her with me, keeping her pressed close.

"Are you alright?" I asked, hoping like hell I hadn't scared her. Hoping it didn't change things between us.

"I'm perfect."

The simple words were enough to calm my fears.

We lay like that for a while, in silence, having said everything we needed to say. And soon, she drifted off. Flush with the energy from her blood, I lay with her in my arms, her breath warm against the crook of my neck as she slept deeply. There were no mutterings under her breath as there had been the last few nights. Whatever was disturbing her had given her peace for one last night.

What I wouldn't give to stay right there, to hold her till dawn and then just pretend that our life together was going to be the forever I'd believed in. My chest hurt, as if I'd been pierced with dragon blood wood.

I lay with her in my arms, her breath warm against the crook of my neck as she slept deeply. The truth of our future battered at my mind and heart, like blows from an unseen enemy.

Sienna was going to die. Maybe not at the battle, but in

time she would die. If I was lucky, very, very lucky, I'd have another fifty years with her. A blip in my life.

If I wasn't lucky?

Something random would take her away sooner. A virus with no cure. A mundane fall in a slippery bathtub. Cancer. Because that was what it was to be human.

The truth of it that I'd been fighting all this time fucking gutted me. I was going to lose her; it was just a matter of time.

I drew Sienna closer to me, as if I could fend off the creep of time by sheer will and pressed my lips against hers. I knew what I had to do. The smile on her lips was fleeting as she reached for me, and I pressed her gently back into the bed.

"Sleep, love."

With a soft sigh she snuggled deep into the spot that I vacated, taking what warmth I left behind.

Slipping from the bed, I dragged on a pair of pants and slipped a shirt over my head.

Fifty years. It would never be enough, but it would be what I aimed for. I made my way to the desk in the room and knew that I had to write the letters. Letters that I'd written before every battle.

But my mind wouldn't leave Sienna, not when the truth of our situation was so painfully clear now. There was no hope of her becoming a werewolf, or a vampire and extending her time with me. She was human, through and through.

The growl that escaped me would have impressed even Lochlin.

So, what to do?

I paced the room, circling the bed, my hands and body wanting to touch her again. To make sure that she was real and alive, and in my bed safe. The time was coming where I was going to have to let her be...not safe.

There might as well have been a sun burning inside my guts. Sienna in harm's way was a horror that I felt through my bones. Could I let her go onto the field of battle, and focus on my own job?

For both our sakes, I had to, or we *would* both end up dead.

"Fuck," I growled as I went to the door that led onto the balcony. The blackout curtains were down, leaving the room in perpetual darkness. As I opened the doors, a wash of salty, cool air flowed in, but it was the sky that drew my eyes.

The moon still hung bright and bulbous, not quite full now as it waned.

But it was the stars, sparking and dancing with their light that I found myself staring at. The moon seemingly overpowered them, but as a cloud scuttled across the orb, the stars shone bright enough that they pushed back the dark.

They seemed so fragile and small compared to the massive light of the moon.

I swallowed hard, knowing that Sienna had to be on the battlefield. She was Starshine. She was the hope in the dark when there was no hope left.

Gripping the edge of the banister, I lowered my head, a shudder rolling through me. Trusting my mate to a fate that I could do nothing to influence was anathema to me. Yet I knew it.

Turning from the balcony, I left the doors open and went to the desk in the room.

There were letters to write.

I penned the first to my mother. She was safe in Verona, for now, but if we lost, she needed to stay there. Edmund would not stop even if I was dead. She knew that, but I wanted her to read it from my own pen. And to tell her that I loved her. That she was a fierce and amazing woman, and because of that, it had taken me a long time to find a woman who measured up to her. I told her about Sienna, and about her strength and heart. Normally, I'd set aside a single sheet for my mother.

I wrote three, somehow feeling that this time was different. That this time...I wouldn't make it. And I wanted my mother to know that I had found the happiness she wanted for me for so long.

Next, I wrote a letter to Will. Told him that he would make a good king even without me there to cuff him when he fucked up. Told him to pull his own head out of his ass and marry Bethany and make some beautiful babies with her. Told him to be happy. To work with Diana and make the world a better place, fix the Veil, simple things.

I'd never penned a note to Lochlin before, but this time I did a quick page for him, thanking him for his friendship, for his willingness to see past species boundaries and for saving my mate. Told him to also pull his head out of his ass and go after the woman he loved finally, because time was not our friend. We didn't have the time we thought we did.

Evangeline was next.

The sound of the sheets slithering to the floor had me turning around. Sienna slid into one of my shirts—it hung to her knees—as she approached me.

"What are you doing up?"

I tapped the pen on the papers. "Before a battle, I leave letters to everyone I love. So they know...in case I didn't tell them."

I rather thought she might be upset at that fatalism I was showing. But she gave a nod. "I think I'd like to do the same. If there's enough paper."

I gave her a few sheets, and she scooped up a pen, then went back to the bed, picking up a book to use as a desk. Her head bowed, long red hair creating a curtain over her face made me wish I had some skill with a paintbrush. She was beautiful in every move she made, but it was her heart that shone through her eyes and her choices. Everything she did, she led with her heart.

My thoughts swirled again toward the battle. Once Edmund realized that she could control the Hunters, that she could connect with them, he'd be gunning for her with everything he had. Will would be forgotten; I would be forgotten. I knew how Edmund thought, and he would see her as the biggest threat.

Once he locked on her, he wouldn't stop until she was dead. Which meant the best protection I could give her would be to go straight for Edmund. Keep his attention on me, and make sure he never saw her power.

Even if it meant my life.

I finished the page to my aunt, paused, and wrote a note to Diana.

The sister I never knew had also made a strong impact on my life in the short time I'd known her.

"Are you writing one for me?" Sienna asked quietly from the bed.

I finished my note to Diana and stood up, going to her on the bed, laying myself next to her and pulling her into my arms. "No. Because there is nothing unsaid between us, Starshine. You have my heart from now until the end of my life, whenever that will be."

She curled against me, the papers she'd been working on crumpling between us. "I wrote one for you."

As I said it, I understood. She thought she would die because she was so vulnerable. That I would be left without her. But I knew the truth. That no matter when she died, I would shortly follow. Even if it meant walking into the sun again. I would not spend a day of this lifetime without her in it.

"We aren't going to be separated, Starshine, where you go, I go." I kissed her gently, unable to look away from her. "Do you understand?"

Her eyes filled with tears. "No, don't say that."

I smiled down at her, calm and peace finally filling me up instead of the fear of her death, and of trying to exist without her.

"My love, you are my reason. Where you go, I go, Starshine. Whether it be into the darkness, or into the light, I am with you."

CHAPTER 19

Sienna

"*Where you go, I go, Starshine. Whether it be into the darkness, or into the light, I am with you.*"

Last night with Dominic was a dream I wished I didn't have to wake from, but morning came quickly. And when I opened my eyes, my contentment was tinged with sadness. Some part of me had hoped, despite knowing it couldn't happen, that I might awaken as a vampire. In reality, it would've been terrible, especially given the timing. I'd have likely been sick like Bethany when I was needed most. But the human heart was selfish sometimes, and just the idea that I might be able to live forever with Dom?

Was a fantasy I couldn't seem to shake.

Feeling decidedly normal, I had to push aside my disappointment and get on with the work of preparing for war. I tried not to think about Dom, or the death and destruction on the horizon, or about the fledgling

Hunter or its mother's pain that had become my own as we gathered and packed our supplies.

We had a job to do, and it was time to dig in and do it.

Despite my mental state, I fell into the rhythm of the work. Hours later, the moment the sun began to slip toward the horizon, we all met in the courtyard to head out.

"Did you leave word with the servants that I'm allowed to stay at the keep?" Myrr called to Diana from the archway. "You know...in case you all die out there?"

Not exactly the last words one wanted to hear from an Oracle, but the Queen took it in stride.

"I did. Everyone knows that you are to be fed and cared for."

Myrr nodded and then ambled back inside, calling over her shoulder, "Ta, then! And good luck!"

Bee came barreling out of the house in a rush, hefting a bag nearly her size over one shoulder.

"Sorry I'm late! I was talking to the wolves in tech and they sent a few more items with us."

"A few?" I asked incredulously. "You look like fucking Father Christmas with that sack."

She raised her brows and shrugged. "It's so weird. It feels

like it weighs almost nothing."

I waited for the jealousy to return with a vengeance, but instead, all I felt was affection and relief. Facing the coming days, battle imminent, it gave me a great sense of peace to know that Bee could handle herself. It wasn't going to be easy, and there was still a good chance we would all die, but at least she wasn't a sitting duck demanding to come along anyway.

"Like you?" a little voice inside my head whispered.

I shoved it aside and continued ribbing Bee. "Well, better go back inside and see if you can grab a few more things, then. Maybe a toaster, or some bowling balls?"

"Har har," she murmured, the glint in her eyes fading as Will and Dom came into sight.

Will didn't even spare her a glance as he passed and Bee drooped visibly, like a flower without sunshine.

Dominic and I locked eyes, and he shrugged. I'd asked him to talk to Will in hopes of getting the young prince to listen to reason, but apparently, it hadn't worked. Under normal circumstances, I'd have left it well enough alone. They were adults and either they'd work things out in their own time, or they wouldn't. Now, though, none of us had that luxury.

I plugged both pinkies into the corners of my mouth and let out a piercing whistle that had Bee jerking her head up in surprise.

"William Blackthorne! Stop right there!" I demanded, stalking toward him, too irritated to care that I was speaking to him like I was the one in line for the crown. Clearly, I played the part well because he slowed to a stop and turned.

"What is it, Sienna?"

His bloodshot eyes met mine and, for a second, I almost felt sorry for him. Not sorry enough to stop, though.

"You," I snapped at Bee. "Drop the sack. Both of you, follow me."

I didn't wait to see if they listened. I just muttered a prayer under my breath and crossed the courtyard over to the gazebo. It was surrounded by dead flowers that would likely be in bloom this time of year if the weather hadn't been on a psychotic rampage. Still, even without the added romance of tulips and daisies, it was a quiet place for them to talk and hopefully come to some sort of resolution.

Once I climbed the few steps of the gazebo I turned and let out a sigh of relief to see them moping their way in my direction like a pair of schoolchildren on their way to the principal's office.

I waited until they joined me before leaping onto my high horse and taking it for a trot.

"You two are acting like idiots, which is fine," I said, my voice shrill as I ramped up. "I act like an idiot most of the time. But we're on our way to a war that is not exactly looking good, and there are only two ways this can go. Kill or be killed. I don't know about you, but as unpleasant as it sounds, I'm gunning hard for option A. Can I safely assume you both feel the same?"

Will opened his mouth to speak but then snapped it shut and just nodded.

Bee, however, shook her head. "Sienna, it's fine. If he doesn't want to talk to me—"

"No! Answer the question. Do you want to live, Bee?" I demanded, glaring at her.

She jutted her chin out mulishly and then shrugged. "Yeah, okay? Yes. But what does that have to do with—"

"If you are both too busy sulking around like a couple of bitch-babies, how in the fuck are you going to be able to focus on the task at hand?"

Bee opened her mouth again and I stuck my finger in it and hooked her cheek like a fish.

"What the hell, Sienna?!" she spat, jerking away, and staring at me like I'd lost my mind.

"You just proved my point. You're a freaking vampire now, Bethany. And you were so preoccupied with all this nonsense with Will that I, a criminally slow human being, got the drop on you. Imagine if I was Scarlett? Or Edmund? I could've just poked both your eyes out and ate them like a pair of Kalamata olives."

Will wrinkled his nose. "Vampires don't...we would never do that."

"Whatever! The point is that, until the two of you work this out, your hearts and minds aren't going to be fully engaged in the most important task of your lives. So, let's get it all out. Right here, right now." I rolled one hand over the other. "I'll get you started. Bee, Will feels guilty because he effectively made you into a monster, however unintentionally. Is that right, Will?"

At first, I thought he might just call the whole thing off and walk away but eventually, he let out a sigh. "Yes. I feel like I...I don't know. Like I stole her humanity from her."

"Say it to her, Will," I encouraged, gesturing to Bee.

He looked at her—really looked at her—for the first time since she'd been able to get out of bed, his tortured eyes drinking her in.

"I'm so sorry, Bethany. If I'd known there was even a chance that could happen, I never would've done it..."

"And if I'd known exactly what would happen, I'd have begged you to," she replied, moving to stand before him and taking his hand. "Will, this was a blessing. Now I can help fight this war. Now I can be part of the solution instead of a hindrance. And best of all?" She stepped closer, until her face was only inches from his. "We can be together...if you still want me."

His expression was pained, but he didn't pull away. "I always wanted you. I just keep thinking about how close you came to death. Bee, there were moments when your pulse was pounding so fast...your heart working so hard that I thought it would explode. I did that to you. Me," he managed through gritted teeth. "The man who is supposed to love you, and I caused you all that pain."

Tears sprang to Bee's eyes.

"Love is pain sometimes, Will. Just like life. You can't grow roses without some fertilizer. That doesn't mean you just stop trying. You have to, like, embrace the shit. You know?"

Will's lips twitched and the tightness in my chest began

to subside.

"Okay, I think you guys got this from here. I'm going to go see if I can fit some more stuff in Bee's bag. Meet you back in the courtyard in a few."

Neither of them even glanced my way.

"Good talk," I murmured as I headed back to where the others were packing saddlebags and filling canteens.

"How did it go?" Dominic asked, pausing to eye me quizzically.

"Pretty good, I think. I left, but I'm pretty sure they're hammering it out."

Loch, who was a few yards away loading arrows into a pack, snickered.

"I bet they are, lass. If we're quiet, we can probably hear them."

"You're a dirty old goat, Lochlin," I replied with a *tsk*.

Not that he was wrong. They could very well be bumping uglies in the gazebo for all I knew. I just hoped they made it a quickie, because, well, war and all...

Diana made her way toward us and turned to Dominic. "The sun will be fully set in less than five minutes. We need to get on the road the moment it does. Barring any setbacks, with time built in for rest and watering the horses, that gives us a two-hour buffer to cross the border and be under the shield's protection before the sun rises."

Two hours was a solid buffer for people trying to make sure they got to a concert early enough to find parking and get to their seats before the opening act went on. It seemed pitifully short when the lives of so many of our people were on the line...including my Dominic.

Still, there was no help for it.

"I'll go get Will and Bee," Dominic said, but before he could make a move, the pair was rounding the corner...

Hand in hand.

Bee was beaming, and Will?

He looked like he'd gotten a last-minute stay of execution. Relieved. Grateful. Afraid, but hopeful.

"Ah, well. Looks like my chance has passed."

I turned to see Raven shaking his head in disappointment.

"Alas, I'll just have to find someone else to lick my...wounds..."

"Your wounds will be just fine," Dominic replied, rolling his eyes. "Now saddle up. We've got to get a move on."

Ten minutes later, we were on our way. For the first

few hours, we rode hard. The weather was cool but comfortable, the moon and stars shone bright, and the trip was blessedly uneventful. I took turns between riding beside Dominic, Will, and Bee, and falling back to chat with members of the Killian clan. Part of me wished I could've talked at least Elka and Kavan out of coming. Jordan would want them home safe with Maya, but I knew I'd have about as much luck as they would have had of talking *me* out of it.

Kavan was the alpha of his—*our*—clan, and as such, he would not be deprived of his pound of flesh. And, as far as I could tell, Elka was a badass bitch who really loved her adopted little brother.

"I meant to give this to you the other night in the great room," she said, closing the distance between our horses and holding out a green, velvet bag. "I found it when I was cleaning out his room. It was with all the rest of ours, and at first, I thought it was our cousin Ailsa, but then I saw the golden eyes and the S..."

My throat went tight as I tipped a tiny figurine into my palm. Like Elka said, I could see by the light of the moon that my eyes were painted gold, and my hair was a deep red, but it was the S that did me in. It was that same shade of red and set inside of a gold triangle dead in the middle of my chest.

Like Superman.

"He loved superheroes. Batman, Antman, The Hulk. But I swear, he thought you could take them all on. He used to tell me stories of how you used to protect him. Like that one time some arsehole was on him at a baseball game, and you hauled off and kicked him right in the man-berries," she said with a low laugh that ended on a broken sob. "Gods' fucking sake, Sienna. Why him? He was so good. Right to his very soul, he was so good. I think about what she did to him, the pain she caused him, and it keeps me awake at night. I can't sleep, I can't eat. She stole something so precious. How could she do that to us?"

I tucked the keepsake back into its bag and then slipped it into my pocket, taking a moment to get a grip before replying. She wanted to talk about him. I got it. Everyone grieved differently, and I wished I could help her.

But the last thing I wanted to think about right now was Jordan. I'd managed to whisk him away, into a box in the back of my mind, to be retrieved if and when we avenged him and survived this war. Then, and only then, would I take the time to grieve him properly.

Time passed so differently here in the Alpha Territories. Bonds that took years to form back home seemed to take hold so much faster here.

So much stronger.

In the mundane world of work and play, caught up in social media and TV, and all the silly trappings of success, did we not feel as deeply or care as much? Or was it that trading in Netflix and reality TV for escaping krakens and staging coups had made us realize what was truly important?

Whatever the case, I knew that Jordan had formed a deep bond with his family in less than a year's time and that bond was as true as ours had ever been.

"He talked to me about you as well, you know," I said softly, absently rubbing Havoc's neck. "He said that you were just as protective of him as I was, and that you beat up one of your male cousins for messing with him. For what it's worth, he really loved you all so much."

"Which is why we need to take this bitch down, Sienna." Elka reached out and tugged on Havoc's reins, pulling to a stop beside me. Her dark eyes glinted like chips of onyx as she held my gaze. "Swear it to me here and now. If we both make it to meet her in battle, we take her down together."

"I swear it. Unless we risk her getting away or hurting someone else, we take her down together."

She held out her hand and I extended mine.

"It's a promise, then," she said as she gripped my forearm and held on tight. "For Jordan."

I could not...I *would* not let them down. I was still picturing Jordan's smiling face when Elka's grip tightened as her fingers grew into claws.

"Did you truly think I'd make it so easy, Corumbra?"

CHAPTER 20

Dominic

"There's the deep woods, and right on schedule," Diana said, slowing her horse to a walk so Ares and I could pull up beside her. "Once we get a little way in, we'll water the horses and see if Sienna can make contact with the Hunters to pinpoint their location."

I nodded, wishing I could spare Sienna that. She'd been shaken to the core by her last interaction with the mother Hunter. But there was no question that it needed to be done. I needed to step back and let her do what she'd clearly been destined for, no matter how much I hated it.

I shot a glance over my shoulder and searched the dozens of faces behind me with a frown. She'd been toward the back of the pack, chatting with Elka not two minutes before.

"Bloody hell," I growled, pulling away from the group.

"What is it?" Diana asked.

"Sienna and Elka have fallen behind. I told her to stay

where I could see her, but the blasted woman is just so stubborn. She refuses to listen."

"Maybe they needed a potty break?"

"They should've held it like the rest of us." I urged Ares into a trot and made my way down the line of horses and riders.

"Where are you going?" Will asked, frowning as I went past.

"To get Sienna to ride up front with me."

But as I reached the end of the line, I realized she was nowhere to be found.

I tightened my legs hard around Ares' barrel and sent him lurching forward as blood pounded in my veins.

"Sienna?" I shouted, scanning the landscape we'd just crossed. "Elka!?"

The sound of hooves behind me had me wheeling back around. Had I somehow missed her? But it was only Loch, Kavan, and a couple of other members of clan Killian.

"When was the last time any of you saw Sienna or Elka?" I demanded.

"They were riding beside me a few minutes ago," Kavan said with a frown. "They canna have gone far..."

"Bloody hell."

My gums tingled and my fangs distended as I leapt off Ares' back. Horses were better for long distance, but I was faster on foot. I found Havoc less than a hundred yards back, pawing the ground, tossing her head, and snorting wildly. She had four deep claw marks down her neck and thick, red blood was pouring from her wounds. Dread settled in my chest as I frantically searched for some sign of Sienna.

And then there she was.

Another fifty yards away, flat on her back. A half-woman, half-wolf was crouched over her, clawed hands wrapped around Sienna's neck in a death grip.

I sprang forward, legs churning under me. When I was within striking distance, I launched myself in the air. Before I reached my intended target, I hit a brick wall and tumbled to the ground, rolling once and springing to my feet.

A massive gray wolf stood between me and the women, ears pinned back, lips quivering as a low growl rumbled from its chest.

"Kavan! Stop!" Loch called as he sprinted toward us. "I dinna know what's wrong with Elka, but she needs to be stopped. We need Sienna if any of us are to survive."

The wolf backed up by inches, keeping himself between me and Sienna, which I wasn't having. I didn't care who the motherfucker was.

I dove for him, but he jerked to one side at the last second and I went hurtling through the air, only to land on empty ground. By the time I got my bearings back, he was just feet from Sienna and Elka.

A bellow ripped from my chest, and I closed the distance between us in one move, but I was too late. Kavan's wolf had already tackled Elka, tossing her to the side and pinning her to the ground with his massive paws.

"Don't hurt her," Sienna rasped, struggling to sit up as she clutched her throat. "She can't help it. She doesn't know what she's doing."

I spared a glance at father and daughter, relieved when Loch joined them, helping a struggling Kavan control his screeching daughter who seemed to be locked in that space in between wolf and human.

"Are you alright?" I asked, lifting Sienna into my arms, and scanning her face and body for more injuries. "Fucking hell, she tried to kill you."

"It wasn't her," she managed, wrapping her arms around my neck, her body trembling. "It was...whatever that being is that spoke through the bloodworm. Dom, I think it's a woman. A she-devil or something. She's unbelievably powerful. I could see it in Elka's eyes even while she was choking me. She tried to fight it. Please...don't punish her. She's a good person, and she loved Jordan. She's just another victim in this."

"What dream?" I growled.

Sienna paled. "It...slipped my mind in all the chaos."

Her next words flowed quickly, and yet chilled me to the core. A dream where in the same voice had spoken to her through Jordan's image, and fought to manipulate Sienna even then. This was getting deeper than I could have imagined.

Elka continued to howl and scream as more of her clan members gathered around.

"Put me down. Please," Sienna begged. "You can come with me. They have her immobilized. I need to try to get through to her."

More than anything, I wanted to ignore her. To follow my own instincts and sweep her off into the forest so we could travel the rest of the way, just the two of us. There was only one person I could trust with her, and that was me. But those damn eyes...

I could deny her nothing.

"Where you go, I go, Starshine," I whispered, setting her down gently.

Together, we made our way to where Kavan and Loch still had Elka spread eagle on the hard-packed earth.

I held onto Sienna's arm as she approached and leaned in, letting Kavan see her.

He didn't try to stop her as she bent low, until she was only a couple feet from Elka.

As much as I wanted to stay angry and full of hatred toward the woman, the agony on her face even as she fought to escape her captors struck a chord in me. Sienna was right. It was like she was literally being torn in two.

"Elka," Sienna whispered. "It's me. Your friend, Sienna."

"Friend?" she snarled as she stopped struggling, her mouth twisting into a leer. "I should hope not. We all know what happens to your friends, don't we, Corumbra? Tell me, how many are you heralding off to their deaths this time? A dozen? A hundred? This is all your fault, you know..."

She visibly flinched, the cruel words hitting Sienna like an onslaught of tiny razor blades.

"No. No, it's not my fault. It's Edmund..."

"If you hadn't come here, we wouldn't be at risk of the Veil being healed. I wouldn't have needed Edmund to do my bidding. Everything could've just gone on as always until it unraveled all on its own. But no," Elka hissed, her face rippling and writhing, no longer human but no longer wolf, either. "You had to come and cause all this trouble. That's why Jordan is dead. That's why all the rest of them will die."

Sienna bit her lip, tears springing to her eyes, but she swiped them away. "Elka, listen to me. I know you're in there. Please come back to us..."

She reached down to her chest and tugged the crest pinned there hard enough that it tore a piece of fabric off with it.

"We're clan Killian. Me, you, and Jordan. He would want us to work together. To be a family. *His* family." She leaned closer and I stiffened, resisting the urge to drag her away. But Elka stayed stock still as Sienna pressed the pin into Elka's clawed hand.

"That's Jordan's pin. We're going to avenge his death. You and me...we made a deal."

Elka's eyes pleaded silently, her body squirming and

jerking even as her mouth moved.

"Don't say I didn't warn you fools..."

Black smog swirled around us, flying out of Elka's mouth, and suddenly Elka dropped back, her body limp and instantly beginning to shift back to her full, human form.

"Son of a bastard," Lochlin said, rocking back onto his heels and pressing his fingers against his temples. "What the bloody fuck was that?"

The hell if I knew, but the bitch was on the top of my shitlist now.

Bending low, I lifted Sienna into my arms again, and left Kavan and the Killians to care for Elka.

By the time we reached a clearing in the deep thicket of woods, nearly an hour had passed since the incident between Elka and Sienna. I'd finally stopped quaking with rage and could almost imagine a world where I didn't want to rip the female wolf's fucking head off for daring to mark my mate.

Progress.

Everyone in our party had done their bit to help set up a makeshift camp, and we'd managed to get several fire pits going under the thick cover of the forest canopy. The scent of roasting meat filled the air, and for a moment, things felt...normal. Like we were just out on a camping trip like some humans from Vermont or something. Then I looked around at the weeping willow trees so similar to those at the funeral grounds, that surrounded us, moving and writhing as they comforted a sobbing Elka, and I scratched that thought.

"I can't help but wonder, why her?" Diana asked, speaking in a hushed tone as she warmed her hands by the fire. "Elka is a strong wolf, but of those in our party, she is middle of the pack at best. Why not pick someone who had the best odds of taking you out easily, like Dominic, or even me?"

Sienna shook her head slowly as she ran her hands over Havoc's neck, the wounds that Elka inflicted sliding into nothing, not even a scar. "I think the being knew I wouldn't be able to control Elka like an animal when she was in that half-state, especially while under duress. I can't say for sure why she picked her specifically, but Elka has been in a bad way. She and Jordan were really close. I get the sense she was his confidant and vice versa, so his death has hit her really hard. She mentioned she hasn't been sleeping or eating. I think the creature sensed her weakness and was able to take possession of her more easily for it."

She paused to run her hands over Havoc and hand her off to one of the stable lads, and I took advantage of the silence.

"And what's to stop her from doing it again?" I demanded, wanting to be understanding...wanting to show the woman some empathy, but wanting my mate to be alive more than either of those things.

"Again, this is still just guesswork, but I feel like she can't maintain control of another person for that long. Either it requires too much energy, or maybe it's like me with the Hunters. If they're too far away, it's difficult to make contact. Whatever the case, she's lost the element of surprise now, and she wasn't successful even when she had it. She's a cunning beast. She'll go back to the drawing board before she shows herself again."

"I'm glad you're so confident. I wish I was," I said, slipping my arm around her waist and pinning her close. How many times would I have to almost lose her? Surely, our luck would run out eventually.

But not today.

"No matter what you think about it, though, no more going rogue. I know I won't be able to have you within arm's reach every moment once we're in the heat of battle, but for the rest of the journey, where you go, I go."

And this time, I meant that as literally as a person could.

"Okay, but—"

It was Diana who cut her off.

"But nothing, Sienna. Without you, we are all doomed. You'll stay by Dominic's side of your own accord, or I'll have one of my men chain you there. We're not going to lose you before we even get to the border."

The Queen's tone brooked no argument, and, to Sienna's credit, she didn't offer one.

"I'm going to see how the elder folks are faring and make sure they get some hot food and drink in them," Diana said, rising to stand.

I watched her go and then turned to Sienna.

"We'll be here at least another hour or so while the horses rest. Are you too pissed at me to let me hold you while you nap? I know we didn't get a whole lot of sleep last night."

And she needed the rest more than I did.

"I'm not pissed at you. I get it. It wasn't Elka's fault, but I think I'd have reacted the same as you. Logic takes a backseat when it comes to matters of the heart."

Just as she spoke those words, I caught sight of Will

bending over and whispering something in Bethany's ear. A few seconds later, the two of them melted away into the darkness.

Sienna set down her skewer and let me pull her between my legs to rest against my chest. I nuzzled her hair, breathing in her scent as she settled in. It only took a few minutes before her breathing went soft and even.

That was good. She needed to recharge from the skirmish we never saw coming. I wouldn't make that mistake again.

Everyone—and I meant everyone—was a potential threat. And next time, it didn't matter how pissed at me she got.

I wouldn't be stopping to ask questions.

CHAPTER 21

Sienna

I woke with a start, my body aching and sore from falling asleep sitting up, my legs numb and tingling. Dominic's arms tightened around me, and his lips pressed to the side of my face.

"Good timing. They just made the call; we are going in."

Going in.

Going to war.

I stood up so fast, the blood rushed away from my head, and I had to take a deep breath to steady myself. I was wearing the leather armor that the werewolves preferred; it was lighter than the chain mail that so many of the vampires wore.

The leather was silent as I moved, clinging to my body. Dominic stood next to me and slung a cloak around my shoulders and pulled the hood up to cover my hair.

"Keep your hair hidden, like we talked about."

I nodded, but my attention was not fully on him.

All around me was a steady hum of movement and noise, voices kept low for the most part but all together. It was like being in the middle of a beehive. Men and women moving swiftly to their assigned places, gathering swords, staffs, bows and arrows. No guns during battles for dominance. The Empires of Magic had banned them from the very beginning, when humans had first created them due to the carnage they'd caused. But when I thought of our arsenal...of the things these creatures could do with fang and claw alone, guns were the least of my worries.

The idea of war had been somewhat abstract, but now that it was here, the adrenaline was pumping before I'd even stepped foot in the saddle. Before I'd even picked up my bow and arrow.

Dominic caught me by the arm and held me gently, steadying me even more, drawing my eyes back to him.

"Sienna. Promise me you'll stay where we agreed? The left flank, closest to the trails that bring you back to the keep if...something happens and you need to run for it? As soon as the Hunters are dealt with, you leave. Promise me again."

I knew what he meant by "something" happening. He meant if he was killed. I was just supposed to run away.

I crossed my fingers, went up on my tiptoes, and kissed him before I answered. "I will do all I can to stay safe, Dominic, and to follow the plan. You know that I don't really want to die, right?"

"No joking at a time like this, not about death." He wrapped me in a tight embrace. "I will be right ahead of you, on the left flank. Stay close behind me."

I knew it, he knew it, and yet I could see he had to say it again, like a mantra. He would be there, that he would protect me.

But we both knew that it was my job to protect everyone by stopping the Hunters.

I'd been trying to connect with Jyx, the male that Edmund had control of, since I'd felt his power.

"What if I can't connect with him?" I whispered. "What if I can't reach him?"

Dominic smoothed out my hair. "Perhaps it is not a matter of 'connecting' or being gentle. You didn't connect with the werewolf female on the beach when she was attacking us. It was different than how you have connected with the others. You told me so yourself."

I frowned. "I know...I...I took control of her; I don't like the way it makes me feel. It scares me."

"But..." He stared deeply into my eyes, "Perhaps that is what you will need to do. That thing that you are afraid of most in order to protect the rest of us."

I smiled up at him, though my lips may have wobbled a little. "And the thing that you are afraid of?"

He spoke without hesitation.

"Losing you, leaving you behind while I ride into battle. I don't like it, but I know that it is what is best for us, for our chances at survival. I am trusting in this plan, in you, and in our comrades."

I slowly nodded, feeling that what he was saying held a large amount of truth to it. I hated controlling the creatures I connected with, so I always held back a little. I hadn't with the werewolf female because that had been a dire situation. There had been no choice but to stop her as fast as I could.

This time was even deadlier, with more lives on the line.

I would do all I had to, no matter how much it turned my stomach.

"Stay safe, my love," Dominic crushed me to his chest, and I clung to him, breathing him in. I wouldn't tell him the whole truth of it. About how close I was going to have to get...how dangerous it was. The moment with the werewolf female was burned into my memory banks. I would have to make eye contact, face to face, to truly lock into the Hunter Jyx's mind. And then, I had to hope that I could keep it together long enough to get him to obey me...before he tore me limb from limb.

"I love you," I whispered to Dominic as he was letting me go, his hands trailing over my body. "To the stars and back."

His smile was everything and then he was gone, striding to the front of the left flank. Gathering his soldiers, rousing them for battle. A battle that not all would come back from.

Bethany hurried over to me, her eyes wide and bright, shining with tears recently shed. No doubt she'd said her goodbye to Will.

"We'll stick together, you and me. No matter what."

I nodded, adrenaline beginning to make itself known again as it rushed through my body. Bee was going to be furious with me too, but there was no choice. I truly understood how close I was going to have to be. Hopefully, it would work, and all would be forgiven.

If not?

I'd be dead, so how mad could they be...

I swallowed a semi-hysterical laugh as Diana called us all to attention.

"Let's get into position!"

Bethany leapt up onto her horse, literally springing onto his back like a damn cat, which sent it skidding sideways, wide-eyed and spooked. I shook my head and mounted Havoc, turning her into position, nodding at Lochlin who was three rows of soldiers over from me. Then I glanced toward Elka, who was just on the other side of Raven. She wouldn't meet my eyes. My body ached from where she'd tackled me, but I'd understood it truly wasn't her fault.

The one behind all this was to blame.

The demon-spawn bitch, hell bent on making sure the Veil was never restored.

Before we could deal with her, we had to deal with the Hunters, Edmund's army, and the Vile King himself.

"One step at a time," I whispered.

I gripped at Havoc's reins and forced myself to let out a breath. All around me werewolves and vampires were lining up for the first charge. Dominic's broad back was at the front of the left flank. Looking to the right, I saw Will in the center, and far to the right was Diana. Three companies, all with one goal.

Destroy Edmund as fast as they could. Because of his cruelty, we were sure if we cut the head off of the beast and dealt with the Hunters, the rest would fall like a house of cards.

Luckily, we had the advantage of surprise this time. Edmund wasn't expecting us to abandon the relative safety of Werewolf Territory and face him and his army, not with the Hunters at his side. We had trustworthy intel that he was planning to send the Hunters in to attack in the morning, forcing our small company of vampires into the sun and diminishing our numbers before following with his men at dusk.

Best that I could tell, the female Hunters had done all they could to slow Edmund down, dragging back, fighting amongst each other, and fighting back against Jyx. Edmund had finally given up pushing them at a distance and brought his army to ride along behind the Hunters, driving them by every means necessary.

Like threatening the remainder of their precious eggs.

Rage and unchecked grief surged through me, and my vision blurred. In a rush, I saw through the female Hunter's eyes, saw the layout of the North Tower. The open field. Felt her turn her head toward me, a connection that had never truly broken after I'd shared in her grief.

Edmund's men were not ready for a battle, they were settling down for the night. Thinking that the Hunters were going to attack us at dawn.

"We're coming," I whispered to the wind, knowing that she could feel my energy. Sense the meaning behind my words. "We will stop him."

Her low rumble of approval sent a shot of energy spiking through me.

A series of owl hoots, and the cries of various night birds and animals cascaded down the line of our army. Dominic's fist shot into the air and then he spread his hand wide and motioned his contingent forward.

I glanced over at Bethany who was shaking hard enough that her reins were smacking against her horse's neck. I reached over and put a hand on her arm. "Take a breath and slow down. Remember, we won't be in the thick of it."

At least, she wouldn't.

No one would be able to keep up with Havoc once we took off.

That's what I kept telling myself, even as the army ahead of us began to pick up speed. Trotting first. Bethany and

I were further back on the left flank, with our own small cadre of fighters. Raven had stayed with us, as had Elka, Rafe, and Jack.

Each of us had our orders.

Rafe, Jack, and Elka were the first line of defense. Then Raven. If Raven fell, it was down to me and Bethany. We were supposed to run for it. But I knew that there was no running. Not this time.

Do or die had never held so much meaning to me as it did in that moment.

The army was at a full gallop now as they broke cover from the trees and out into the open fields that lay surrounding the North Tower.

Raven, Rafe, Jack and Elka were just in front of me and Bethany.

"Bee?" I said just her name and she glanced at me, her eyes incredibly wide. I smiled. "I need you to trust me, okay?"

"Of course, but...why?" Her wide eyes narrowed so fast that I thought for a moment she'd closed them. "Sienna."

"Just...trust me?"

The bellow of the Hunters ripped through the pounding hooves.

I tightened my hold on Havoc's reins, speaking just loud enough for those around me. "Be ready, all of you."

"Lady, we're supposed to stay back," Rafe said with horror in his voice. He did not want to be here, despite his training.

Another bellow of the Hunters as they could see the oncoming army first and sounded the warning. It was surreal to watch our forces approach through the Hunter's eyes overlaid with my own vision.

"I have to be closer than I realized. I need to lock eyes with the largest male." I felt a shiver as the female Hunter looked not to her left, but to the far right. That's where Jyx was, just waking up from a nap, apparently.

To the far right. As far from Dominic as he could be.

Well fuck me.

Dominic would kill me if we survived this. "The big male Hunter is on the far right. We have to join Diana's flank. Now! Don't argue. Either you go with me, or I go it alone."

Raven grunted. "I knew you were trouble." He hesitated, and then shook his head in reluctant agreement. "Fine, we will do our best to keep everyone off you. If it goes well, you won't even see us."

I didn't give him a chance to say more. Jyx was starting toward Diana and her contingent, and I could *not* let him reach her. He spread his wings and roared, shattering the world with his bellow.

No time. There was no time...

I leaned forward, urging Havoc into a full tilt gallop, turning her to the right, cutting across the back of the army.

There was no time to wait to see if my bodyguards were able to keep up with me. No time at all if I was going to save Diana and her fighters. I gave Havoc her head and the black mare stretched out as we came tearing around the furthest right side of the right flank. Full tilt, I didn't even think to slow her down, just raced past the soldiers who were focused on the massive Hunter bearing down on them, his head and open mouth headed straight for my friends.

His wings were unfurled, the wind off them buffeting the front of the army. I tried reaching out to him with my mind.

Nothing.

Fucking hellfire, this was bad. Bumping Havoc's sides with my heels, I urged her faster yet, overtaking the front of the contingent. I caught a glimpse of Diana as I passed her.

"No!" she screamed as I flashed by, but there was no stopping me now.

Do or die.

I was in front of everyone, with nothing but leather for protection, and no weapons but the whip at my side, and the bow and arrow that was strapped to the back of my saddle.

None of that mattered.

"Hey, you great big bastard!"

I sat back and Havoc slid to a stop, rearing up as if she would fight the massive Hunter on her own. Honestly, I wouldn't have put it past her, she had the heart for it.

The Hunter didn't slow his trajectory, but his gaze *finally* swung my way, narrowing on me.

I held up a hand and stared up into his crimson eyes, the hatred in them running deeper than anything I'd ever encountered. He shot toward me, mouth gaping wide, but I still had his eyes in sight.

"No," I whispered the word, sending that energy through the tentative connection between me and the Hunter.

He bellowed his anger, slowed his attack, but didn't pull

his gaze away.

The rage that pulsed through him was a palpable thing, coating every inch of my body. Diana reached my side, and I thought she'd tell me to get back, but she didn't.

She let out a howl that meant so many things.

Attack.

Protect.

Defend.

I felt it through to my bones even as I held that Hunter still. The army spread out around us, fighting off Edmund's men while I dealt with Jyx.

I couldn't make him back down like I could the females. But I could keep him from attacking. I could hold him steady, and then the females would stay out of the fight too.

There was screaming all around me, and the connection to the male Hunter's mind deepened, which made the rest of the world fall away...the sound softened, as if the battle were distant instead of right in front of me.

It was like flipping through a book of photographs, seeing the Hunter's life through glimpses of images. Hatching. Stolen from his mother. The collar being placed on his neck. Training with Edmund.

Fuck, the training made me want to vomit, the agony and torture he'd been put through until he was no better than Edmund himself, a monster who fed on death and pain. There was no coming back for him, any more than there was coming back for Edmund.

There was no fixing the breaks in his psyche.

Jyx bellowed and my body shivered with the force of it. I clung to the edge of the saddle, nails driving into the hardened leather. Havoc stood stock still, unfazed by the Hunter in front of her.

His voice boomed through me.

You would kill me.

"I would set you free if I could," I said through grit teeth, the images of his past still flickering in me.

Then you would all die. I am a creation of my master. You see that truth now.

It was so strange, the calm in which his mind spoke to mine.

He controls my impulses, my every aspect of being. There is no safety as long as I am alive.

"I can't..."

There are other eggs. Protect them, Corumbra. Kill me, and set my mates free of the pain that I have caused them.

Sorrow, thick like rancid honey coated my senses and I nearly lost the connection to him. I blinked and fought to lock my eyes on his again, staring straight into the depths, seeing behind the red, to the deep blue that they'd once been.

You must do it. It is the only way.

Even as he spoke calmly, his body bellowed and thrashed in the air, fighting to get away from me, his head unmoving though, as if I had a lock on it.

He was right, I could feel the truth of it as surely as I felt his rage.

I didn't close my eyes but let myself sink deeper into the red madness that his orbs contained, past the once blue eyes. Deeper and deeper through him until I found the part of his mind that controlled...everything. The part that Edmund also held tight.

The fighting was ramping up all around me. There were arrows flashing through the air, swords crashing against shields, the hum of an ironwood staff not far from me. But all of it had to remain distant.

With a cry of sorrow, I plunged deep into the part of his mind that made his heart beat, that made his blood pump. I pushed Edmund out, slicing that connection first.

Freeing the Hunter from his master so at least he would die unchained.

And then I...I...stopped it all. It was like flicking off a light switch, a really big, rusted light switch. It took all my concentration and effort. Pain cut through me like a blade, I screamed as I forced it all to stop, because I felt that last second of life, the last breath and heartbeat and it was my fault that it was no more.

Despite everything, I grieved for him, for what could have been.

Jyx was flying, hovering above the army one second, and the next, his entire frame seized, his eyes widened, red flashing to blue in his last second as he went down, sending soldiers flying, blocking part of our path to the North Tower.

There was a moment of eerie silence and then a cheer went up from our side, the army seeing it happen, knowing that I had done it. Of course, that meant that Edmund and his men...

They'd seen me do it too.

"KILL HER!" Edmund's voice shattered the air like nothing else could have, but I was not done yet. He was trying to direct the other Hunters, but they disregarded him.

I felt their thoughts pressing on my mind, and I sent them one back.

Flee, while you can...protect your eggs.

They lifted off and there was a moment that I was sure Edmund thought I was going to die. But the female Hunters flew over me, tipping their wings in salute, one at a time.

All but one.

The one whose egg had been broken, the one whose pain I shared. She landed in front of me and bowed her head.

We destroy him...together.

CHAPTER 22

Dominic

The thrum of the battle kept all my attention forward, as much as I was leaving my heart behind me with Sienna. I'd ridden away quickly, because if I didn't turn away, I wasn't sure I'd be able to.

To leave her behind took every bit of fortitude I had in me. To trust in others for her protection was a rank sore in my gut.

Lochlin rode up next to me. "Into the darkness once more, let us be the light and kick them in their motherfucking bollocks."

I snorted. "Almost poetic, my friend. Almost."

Lochlin grinned. "I do what I can to bring beauty to even the most difficult of moments."

The men around us laughed, and I lifted my hand, fist over my head. The call of the birds was our signal. I flexed my fingers and flicked my wrist forward.

Into the battlefield we went.

Ares plunged and danced, wanting to break into a flat-out gallop, but we needed to get clear of the last big line of trees first. The trot picked up speed until we burst out of the forest's edge to see the North Tower ahead of us. Draped over the top of the tower to the far right was Jyx, the massive male Hunter. He didn't even glance our way, his gaze trained on Diana's contingent.

I couldn't help but breathe a sigh of relief. The further the Hunters were from Sienna, the better. She would be safer this way.

The less likely Edmund would realize that she could stop them.

"For William, and the throne!" I roared the words, knowing it would draw ire our way. My fangs descended as we leapt into a gallop, rushing toward the unsuspecting army. Our spies said that he didn't even have scouts or guards set out, he was relying solely on the Hunters to do all the heavy lifting for him. They were settling down for the night, not ready for an attack.

Lochlin was beside me, his body twisting in mid-air as he took on his wolf shape, keeping up with Ares better than I thought. The massive ginger wolf let out a howl, and half our contingent took up his cry.

Part of the plan was to create as much chaos and confusion so we could pin the army down—we didn't want to kill them all, just Edmund and those loyal enough to protest when we dispatched him—long enough for me or Will to get to Eddy. To remove his head and end this.

I braced my body, ironwood staff pointed out like a lance as I slammed into the first row of soldiers. The first one I hit went straight into the air and over my back, into the mass of oncoming werewolves.

I jumped off Ares and swung the ironwood staff around me, creating a circle as I put myself in the center of the melee.

Falling into the rhythm, I swept legs out, snapped necks, broke spines and ribs. Despite the effort, I'd never felt stronger. I could thank Sienna and her magical blood for that.

A dagger flew past my face, close enough that I felt the blade slice through the flesh of my cheek.

I spun and faced my next opponent, already knowing before I ever turned who it was. There was only one fighter who'd ever gotten close to killing me in practice.

Scarlett stared at me, her eyes wild, her face twisted into a mockery of a smile.

"So, you'll try and kill me? I know all your moves, General...in *and* out of the sack."

The men around us continued to fight, but I barely noticed them. Scarlett had all my attention now.

"How could you do it? You knew what we were fighting for! Edmund is a fucking monster, you said so yourself!"

Her eyes narrowed. "Did you never wonder how I helped you in those early years? How I always managed to figure out where the attempts on Will's life would happen? I've been fucking him for years, keeping the enemy close—for *you*. But what I didn't realize," she pulled her ironwood staff from her back and spun it lazily in front of her body, stepping sideways, "was that my real enemy was the one I let into my heart."

I shook my head as she swung her staff, faster than I'd ever seen her move. I blocked it and we began the dance that would surely leave one of us dead.

"I never said I loved you," I growled as the two staves began to hum, mine heating up in my hands. "I never led you on."

"Didn't you?" she laughed as she managed to get through my guard and thrust the point of hers into my shoulder, sending me back. I had few weak spots, but she *knew* them. "You never had any other partner but me."

I readjusted my footing and spun my staff across my body, bringing it around to sweep at her feet. She leapt back lightly, fangs flashing. It was as if the battle had all but disappeared around us even as the roars of the male Hunter in the distance grew louder. But if I didn't focus on the here and now, I would be dead and of no use to anyone.

No use to Sienna.

"But you did," I laughed as she turned bright red. "It's why I picked you to fuck and not someone else, because I knew there would be no expectations of me. That I would never be your one and only."

She screamed, rage twisting her features into a person I didn't know, if I'd ever known her at all. Scarlett was no longer my friend; she was no longer my comrade in arms.

She was my mortal enemy.

The clash of our staffs against one another threw sparks out around us, lighting the grass on fire in places, adding to the atmosphere of chaos and fear in the night.

The screech of the male hunter ripped through the air, catching my eye as he winged toward the right flank, toward Diana.

"You chose a fucking *human* over me!" Sienna's screech filled the air, slowing more than a few fights.

"I would never have chosen you, Sienna or no Sienna!" I snapped back. "Scarlett, Edmund will kill you the minute you don't do as he wishes. You *know* this. You've seen it a dozen times when he tires of his women!"

We were both breathing hard. This was the problem with fighting someone you knew so fucking well, the fight would go on a long time, drawn out by seeing the moves long before they actually happened.

"I will be his Queen, and his General. I don't care if he fucks everything that moves, as long as I keep my place."

She snarled and snapped her staff around, driving it into my right thigh. I rolled through the blow and realized that killing Scarlett was not going to be easy.

Not for me.

Not even after everything she'd done.

I could have killed her three times over already. And yet...I was hesitating. "Scarlett, even if you survive, William will be king. And you will be executed."

She was about to lunge at me again when Jyx bellowed and then fell from the sky, rumbling the ground, throwing bodies, living and dead, in every direction as he landed.

Edmund bellowed something in the distance, but I couldn't make it out over the wild cheers and screams of pain.

But it hardly mattered. What mattered was that Sienna had dropped the male Hunter. My heart swelled with pride. She stopped Jyx all on her own, at a fucking distance, no less.

I grinned at Scarlett. "My mate is kicking Edmund's ass."

Scarlett took a step back, tears gleaming along with the madness in her eyes.

"You broke my heart, Dominic. And that useless, weak human? She's going to die today if it's the last thing I do!"

She turned away from me and I swung hard at her retreating back, fear striking me like a physical blow. But it was not Scarlett's body or staff that I came into contact with, but the blade belonging to none other than the brother I hated. The one I'd waited so very long to face in true battle.

Edmund bared his teeth at me in his version of a smile.

"How will you survive, with your new toy dead, hmm?" Edmund mocked as Scarlett backed away.

I didn't dare glance behind me and give away Sienna's position, not even to make sure she was safe. I only knew that the Hunters were no longer losing their minds, and Jyx was down, which meant Sienna had done what she needed to do.

Now she would make a run for the Queen's Keep.

Please Sienna. For once, do as you're told and make a run for the fucking Queen's Keep.

"She is not the one dying today, Edmund. I suggest you get ready to make your peace with Father, as you are about to face him once more."

I rolled the staff in my hands and swung it up to catch him in the jaw. He danced back and there was nothing I could do. I couldn't follow Scarlett to Sienna. Not while face to face with Edmund. Luckily, it mattered not. She was headed to the right flank, away from Sienna.

Focusing on Edmund, I put all my effort into taking him down, for the first time unleashing everything I had in me. I drove him back, further, and further, my blows unrelenting.

With one giant backswing of the staff, I removed Edmund's sword from his hand and sent it flying across the battlefield.

"What now, brother?" I asked, chest heaving with exertion as I moved in on him.

He sent me a chilling grin and snapped his fingers.

"Meet my new friends, Nicky. I borrowed them from Damian."

Damian.

The demon king...

The name had a split second to register before a body the size of a horse slammed into me, driving me to the ground. I didn't know what to make of the thing on me. Thing, because it was no vampire, and it was no werewolf.

It was built like a rhinoceros, with a black horn jutting from the center of its head, beady eyes, arms, and legs like tree trunks.

I rolled with the creature and came up with my back to my men.

Or so I thought.

Another creature grabbed me from behind, pinning my arms to my sides and lifting me off the ground, bellowing in my ear, cracking my ribs tight. Hot, fetid breath poured over me, spittle splattering the back of my neck.

I grabbed for the dagger I kept strapped to my arm, yanked it free and jabbed it back into the forearms of the beast. It bellowed and dropped me. I spun and saw Edmund's sword swinging for my head, as if in slow motion.

Even if I threw myself to the ground, I could see that the trajectory of his blade would follow, and I was about to get my head removed from my shoulders. There was no time for fear, or regret. Only for one thought.

Starshine. This would kill her.

An ironwood staff shot between me and the blade, bouncing the sword away at the last second, the glint of metal and ironwood meeting creating a burst of flame.

"Looks like you could use some help, brother?" William said, stepping in between me and Edmund, slowly spinning his staff. "And I have a throne to take."

This was William's moment, as future king, it would be best if he was the one to kill Edmund. Despite my overwhelming desire to lop off our older brother's head, the incoming threat was just as pressing.

"Good. Take it and I'll deal with the demons."

"Demons?"

"Edmund's newest friends," I growled as I turned to face the two behemoths. I put my ironwood staff down and pulled my sword. I couldn't even enjoy watching Will kill Edmund. Not if I wanted to keep my own head attached.

The two demons rushed me at the same time. I ducked

under the swinging hands of the first, stepped and swung up with the blade, lopping off the demon's arm. He bellowed and spun away from me, allowing me to focus on the other. A blow hit my lower back and sent me flying a good twenty feet from the fight. I hit the ground, rolled, and saw the demon headed for Will's back.

There was no time to reach him. I took two steps and threw my sword, using both hands as if it were a throwing axe, and sent it flying through the air, end over end. A moment later, it buried itself into the demon's back, through his heart, all the way to the hilt.

The demon grunted and went down sideways.

"Stupid," a low voice growled at me. "Now you gots no weapon."

I turned to see the first demon still bleeding copiously from the stump of his arm, seemingly unfazed by the wound.

"Don't I?" I growled, showing my fangs, the animalistic side of me taking over in the face of a monster more hideous than any I'd faced in a very, very long time. "There are so many ways to die, demon. Let me show you a new one."

He bent at the waist and roared at me, showing an

impressive number of teeth, but none as sharp as my own.

I dared a glance at Edmund and Will, to see my younger brother driving that bastard back, step by step, the ironwood staff a blur. It hit me in that moment that he'd held back in our sparring. His speed was unreal.

My momentary distraction was enough for the demon. He lurched at me, tackling me to the ground. We rolled over and over, knocking more than one soldier down in our path.

I found his neck and bit hard, tearing sideways and opening up every artery he had. His laughter gurgled out around us.

"You think that'd work, when lopping my arm off didn't?"

The opening I'd created showed me a glimmer of spine.

"Wasn't trying to bleed you out."

The demon reached for my neck with his one hand. But I was faster. I snaked my hand forward, drove it through the remaining flesh of his neck and grabbed hold of his spine. With a heave, I stood and pinned his body with my foot as I yanked, pulling free the accordion of bone and cartilage.

I bellowed, flung the spine and turned in time to see

Edmund sprinting away from Will.

"He runs, the coward!" I yelled. "After him!"

Our men surged forward, and Edmund's army fell back, many to their knees, hands over their heads in surrender.

"Do not kill them!" William shouted. "Bind them."

And then he and I were tearing after Edmund as he ran toward the right flank in the direction Scarlett had gone.

"I couldn't stop her," a low voice called as a figure pulled up beside me.

Raven.

His voice cut through the blood lust pounding in my head.

"Sienna. She took to the right flank, stopped the big Hunter. She wouldn't go back to the keep!"

Sienna was on the right flank...

Right where Scarlett and Edmund were headed.

CHAPTER 23

Sienna

The battle raged around me, but it was as if I didn't exist for those few moments. The female hunter launched herself upward, and I knew why.

She was looking for Edmund. The killer of her hatchling.

I will tear him to pieces.

Bethany raced up to my side, out of breath, horseless, and with a smear of blood across her cheek. "Sienna!"

Relief shot through me as I grabbed her hand and hauled her up onto Havoc's back. One person that I loved was safe.

"Let's go!"

Everything slowed then as Havoc turned to get us off the field of battle. The moment we took that first step, something slammed into us, sending us crashing to the ground with a tremendous, earth-shaking boom, and knocking the wind out of me.

"Sienna, run!" Bethany was up and facing whoever had knocked us over. Havoc grunted and lurched to her feet, shaken, and pissed. I rolled to my knees to see Bethany squared off with Scarlett, Dominic's captain. The Betrayer.

Murderer of Jordan.

"Go, damn it!" Bee commanded, never even looking my way.

Scarlett sneered, and I saw the moment she was going to kill my friend. Just like she'd killed Jordan. But we were not alone. A blur of dark brown fur erupted out of the mass of bodies, and Elka tackled Scarlett to the ground, throwing her away from Bethany.

Not alone.

"We face her together," I said as I pulled my bow and arrow from the saddle. Havoc gave a low snort and pawed at the ground, not to be left out.

Bethany came to my right side, and Elka to my left. "Together," Bee growled.

Elka snarled and crouched, prepared to spring.

Scarlett rolled to her feet and laughed. "Even together, you three cannot beat me. I've spent decades studying the art of war. You are not fighters."

We circled around her, and to anyone looking it would have seemed an unfair fight, but Scarlett was no lady in waiting. Dominic had trained her himself. I had no doubt that we were in for the fight of our lives.

Elka struck first, diving in and going straight for Scarlett's legs. Bee followed and went for Scarlett's upper body. It looked like it might work. My heart beat so fast, I could hear it over the sounds of battle.

Scarlett whipped an ironwood staff across the side of Elka's head, dropping her like a stone, then snapped the point of it back and into Bee's stomach, catching her hard and throwing her through the air, over the heads of the soldiers, far away from me.

Which left just me facing her, my bow and arrow clutched in my hands. I didn't hesitate at least. I loosed the arrow, straight at Scarlett's head. She ducked and I pulled another arrow, set and fired before she could dance back.

"I'm going to rip your face off. See if he wants to fuck you then." Scarlett grinned at me. "There will be no healing that. Then I will let him watch as I tear your heart out and throw it at his feet."

"Tell me how you really feel." I stepped sideways, unfazed by her words. I had to keep moving. I kept firing arrows, as if I were trying to drive her to the left, with her pulling back to the right.

"Dominic!" I turned to see Elka hurling a throwing axe to Scarlett's left, and I recognized it instantly for what it was.

A distraction.

I loosed my last shot, firing to the right as Scarlett feinted away from the axe and stepped directly into the path of my arrow.

Score.

The arrow was dragon blood wood, and it sunk deep into the middle of her chest. Not her heart, but the bellow that ripped out of her told me that it hurt like a motherfucker. I had to hope it would be enough to slow her down.

Or not.

She screamed and then dropped her staff and rushed me, a blur of speed.

Havoc drove between us, rearing up, slamming her iron-hard hooves into Scarlett's shoulders, but not before Scarlett grabbed a front leg and snapped it, like breaking a twig.

"NO!" I screamed and leapt forward, tackling Scarlett.

It was a stupid move, I knew it was, but I couldn't help it. This was the second time Havoc had saved my life. The second time she'd been injured doing it.

Scarlett grinned as she reached for me, like she was going to embrace a lover, her fangs bared.

I brushed against Havoc as I fell toward Scarlett, and a burst of energy and rage ripped through me.

Animalistic.

Havoc was giving me her strength...every last bit she had so that I could defeat Scarlett.

I fell onto Scarlett, driving my fist into the side of her head, twice before she snaked away from me and faced me, her eyes narrowing.

"What—?"

I didn't give her a chance to figure it out. I scooped up the ironwood staff that she'd dropped and swung it toward her like a baseball bat, the staff vibrating in my hand.

It blurred as I put everything I had into the hit. Maybe she thought she had time, maybe she thought that I would pull back. But the connection between the staff and her head was solid, a crack that echoed around us, her body flying through the air.

Her eyes rolled as she hit the ground, miraculously,

getting back up, albeit wobbling as if she'd been on a drunken binge.

Havoc fed me more of her energy, whether I wanted it or not, and I went after Scarlett.

"You aren't hurting anyone else I love, not ever again!"

She shook her head and winced, but it was a cover. She lurched forward, a short blade in her hand.

I blocked it, moving at a speed that I knew came from Havoc. I spun the ironwood like I'd seen Dominic do, rolling it in my wrist, shocked at how light it was.

Scarlett blocked my blow, though I could see she was slower than she had been. The side of her head where I'd hit her, was bleeding, pouring down her neck. The arrow in her chest was quivering.

There could be no quarter given. I jabbed her with the point of the staff, sending her back a few steps and down to one knee. "You killed Jordan."

"Fuck you," she growled. "He was weak. Like you."

"You betrayed Dominic, and broke my horse's leg!" I slammed her in the side, feeling ribs break under the force of my blow. Havoc grunted behind me, and I knew I had to finish this—now.

"He loved me first," she whispered, her eyes filling with

tears, her speed and strength gone with the blows she'd sustained, from the dragon blood wood arrow in her chest. "You stole him from me."

I stood over Scarlett and stared down at her. "I have no pity for you. If you loved him, you would have wanted him to be happy and safe. Instead, you tried to kill him. Tried to give him to his enemy. That's not love."

There was no more time, the battle was shifting around us, the cries of men and their deaths coming back to me. I dropped the ironwood staff and ripped the arrow out of her chest. She screamed and writhed, blood spilling out across her armor. I set the arrow to my bow and aimed at her heart.

She stared up at me, her face going from tears to fury as she lurched again for me. I fired the arrow and it shot true, straight through her heart.

Scarlett's body jerked and she fell at my feet, face down.

It was over, she was gone. I lowered the bow, shaking from head to foot.

A soft whinny turned me around. Havoc lay on her side, just her head raised to me and then she lowered it, a huge sigh sliding out of her.

I ran to her side and laid my trembling hands on her

neck.

"No! You can't leave me now, not now, Havoc."

Her soft whinny tore at my heart. I knew that I should get off the battlefield, I knew that I should go and get to safety—but I couldn't leave her. My first friend in this place, my first defender against anyone who would dare harm me.

The connection between her heart and mine expanded, and I felt my way along her leg. I could heal her. I could do it and then she'd be okay. But even as I thought it, there was something else, something deeper wrong.

"Lady Sienna, we have to go!" Rafe was suddenly there. I noted that he'd shown up after my fight was through.

I couldn't blame him though. He and Jack were young, and I'd seen the terror in their faces...

"Not yet."

I reached for Havoc's...spirit...is that what I was touching when I connected with her and the other animals?

It was as if my understanding opened up, and even as Havoc's heart began to falter, I reached to the closest other creature, one strong enough to share her strength.

The female Hunter swept over our heads, low enough

that I was able to reach up and let my fingers brush along her belly, drawing power from her.

Power.

Magic.

Spirit.

I wove the three together and plunged them into Havoc's failing body, feeling my way to her wounds and healing them. Scarlett hadn't just broken her leg. She'd slashed the mare's belly open too, her insides out on the ground below her body.

"You aren't leaving me, my beauty," I murmured, weaving the power through her, tightening sinew and muscle, binding skin, and putting pieces back together. But there was more that she needed, and I felt the Hunter above me whisper a suggestion.

"Oh, that is an excellent idea." I smiled. I smiled in the middle of a raging battle, trusting the Hunter to have my back. The longer I knelt there, the further my power rippled outward.

I could feel Bethany to my right.

Elka to the left.

Both were stunned, but alive. Diana was further yet, battling three of Edmund's fighters.

Dominic was coming in fast from my left, Will just ahead of him and Edmund himself...

"You sneaky little bitch. I'll kill you myself."

I looked up to see him standing less than ten feet from me, a sword in his hand, dripping with blood.

I felt the connection to the Hunter as she glided in slow circles above to regain the strength she'd so generously offered. I felt Dominic and Will as they closed in on Edmund.

And I smiled some more. I smiled because I knew what he didn't.

That he was about to die.

CHAPTER 24

Dominic

She was alive.

Alive and smiling, no less, despite her every apparent effort to die in battle today. I wanted to rage at her and kiss her senseless all at once, but there was still work to be done.

"Will!" Bethany called, her bloodied face a mask of joy and relief as she stood for an instant and then stumbled to the ground again.

She'd clearly been in the thick of it, and her energy was depleted, but she didn't appear to be mortally wounded. A fact that didn't stop Will from charging toward her first.

"Hold off Edmund until I get them out of reach!" he shouted over his shoulder, gesturing to a struggling Elka as well.

I understood the sentiment. If I thought there was any chance of Sienna staying put, I'd have done the same with her, but I knew better. I shot a glance her way and caught sight of the prone figure a few yards behind her. There, with an arrow protruding from the center of her chest, lay Scarlett.

Motionless.

I'd already grieved her loss when I realized she'd betrayed me. Betrayed our people. Now, I felt nothing but pity and relief. She was a formidable fighter, and her loss weakened Edmund's army in more ways than one. She'd had the respect of her soldiers in a way that Edmund never had. They would fight for her because they had trained and battled together for years. I knew that most only fought for Edmund because they were afraid of what would happen if they didn't.

"Edmund!" I bellowed as I sprinted toward him, cutting him off when he was ten steps away from a still-grinning Sienna. He wheeled around, our swords clashing loudly as they crossed and held tight.

He stared at me; his eyes filled with a hatred that was almost palpable.

"Why do you even care? Why does a bastard who has no claim to the throne even care about any of this?" he snarled before breaking our stalemate and swinging again with all his might.

I blocked his strike and feinted backward before rushing at him with a dizzying array of blows. Only one hit its mark, cleaving the meaty part of his thigh like a roast, but I'd gotten what I wanted. Another few yards of distance between him and Sienna.

"I care because I don't want a black-hearted monster ruling our people. Simple enough."

Edmund took another step back to buy himself some time to regroup, I'd have wagered. Then, he too saw Scarlett's body and stilled. For a second, I wondered if, under all that cruelty, there was a tiny part of his rotten heart that could actually feel.

Then he shrugged.

"Sad. She was very useful...in so many ways. If it weren't for Stirling insisting on you for the job, I'd have made her my General long ago. And she was a good lay, too. But, alas...we move on, yes?"

Very quickly, apparently.

He began to circle me slowly, like the shark he was.

"I have to be honest, I was surprised to hear she was fucking you. You're an excellent guard dog, Nicky. Dumb, strong, and loyal to a fault. But those pesky morals get in the way of you having any fun at all. If you'd just fallen in line, you could've had everything but the crown. Surely more than a bastard deserves."

I shot him a cold smile. "Yeah, well, if we all got what we deserved, you'd have been drowned in the sea as an infant to save the rest of us from your reign of terror, Edmund."

He snarled as he launched himself at me, sword extended, palming the butt of it with his free hand as if to drive it through my heart like a stake. I thought about taking the brunt of his blade in the shoulder while I buried mine into his gut, but opted to move at the last second, sending him stumbling flat onto his face. The sword clattered against a rock and cracked at the hilt, rendering it useless.

Leave it to Edmund. His own sword that I'd separated him from earlier was an indestructible masterpiece, but the blade he'd grabbed from one of his fallen men was of low quality, because fuck them, right? They were expendable. Just like Will. Just like Scarlett. Just like everyone but Edmund, to his mind.

I took a moment to appreciate the irony as he rolled to his feet, weaponless again, face filled with madness and rage.

"Do you truly think I need a blade to kill you, bastard brother, mine? We've both always known if it came right down to it, I could take you, sword or no. Of course, if you think you need yours, by all means…"

The sounds of battle had quieted around us, and I realized with a start that we had an audience. Both armies had heard the challenge. A man to man, hand to hand fight to the death. One that would end all of this in an instant.

I should've ignored it. Gods knew Edmund would have, but I also knew it meant something. I was an extension of Will. It would go a long way towards a smooth transition of power to do this the right way. And if I failed, I trusted that Will would come finish the job for me.

"Dominic…" Raven called from where he and several others watched a dozen yards away, his voice a warning. "Don't let him manipulate you into this. Just end him now."

"Are you kidding?" I called back over my shoulder as I faced off against the vile, soon to be dead, King. "I've been waiting my whole life for this."

I tossed my sword aside and cracked my neck before beckoning him toward me.

"Let's go, asshole."

He grinned.

"You again with those pesky morals. Such a Boy Scout."

In a flash, he swiped a throwing knife from his boot. It was like it was happening in slow motion. One second, he had his wrist cocked with a deadly aim at my chest, the next, there was this sudden *crack* followed by a howl of pain as the knife fell to the ground and blood spurted from his wrist.

He whipped his head around to glare at Sienna, who stood nearby, nostrils flaring with fury, whip in hand.

"You meddling bitch," Edmund hissed as he dove for my discarded sword. I was about to beat him to the punch when Sienna called my name, her voice shrill with fear.

"No! She's coming for him...stay back!"

From behind me, I could hear the Hunter's wings whooshing through the air as she approached. As much as I'd wanted to kill Edmund with my own two hands, he would die today. And that would be enough.

The screech from above was deafening, and I slapped my hands over my ears as the sky seemed to go dark. The female Hunter's body blocked the sun as she swooped in and struck Edmund's body and tore out his entrails with her razor-sharp claws.

He howled in agony as she flew away, desperately clutching at his belly, trying to hold himself together to no avail. I could see the very moment that he knew it was futile. He would not live to see another day. But instead of raging, he used his last bit of strength to reach into his pocket.

"If I go, I'm taking the rest of you with me," he managed, his voice already weak and raspy.

Another screech rent the air as the Hunter made her second pass. I watched Edmund's eyes as they registered an instant of shock and terror before she ripped his head from his body in one, clean strike.

Silence fell over the battleground, so all-encompassing that, when a bird dared to chirp, the sound was deafening.

It was done. Edmund the Vile was dead.

Now all that remained was the aftermath.

"Dominic," Will's low voice called to me. "The shield…"

It took a few seconds for his words to register, but when they did, my blood ran cold. I looked to the sky in horror as our protective shield slowly dispersed.

"Get to the tower, all of you, now!" I shouted, already feeling the heat.

The screams were unlike anything I'd ever heard as my

brethren felt the sun's first deadly rays and pandemonium ensued. Vampires running as fast as they could to get to the stone tower in the distance, but their speed was like that of a human as the sun did its best to kill them on the spot.

"Most won't make it, Dom!" Sienna screamed even as she ran toward me. "Save yourself!"

Searing pain made it hard to think as I leapt into action, sprinting to Will even as he sprinted away from me.

"Bethany!" he yelled, running with all his might in the opposite direction of the tower.

Damn it all to hell.

I used it all—the agony of burning...the fear of seeing hundreds of my kind killed in the most cruel, gruesome way...the fury at Edmund for his last, evil parry—I used every bit of it to propel me forward, leaping the final distance between my brother and tackling him at the knees.

"No, damn you. Get off! As your king, I command you to get the fuck off me!"

He twisted and jerked like a bronco, but I held tight, using my larger body to shield his as I pinned him to the ground.

In that moment, the pain ceased, and all I felt was peace

tinged with regret for what could have been.

My brother would live. The wolves and Diana would come to shield him, whisk him to safety once they realized what had happened.

My woman would live. Taking blood from her hadn't made her one of us. And, despite her bitter disappointment, that would be the very thing that would spare her.

That was the sweet.

But suddenly those fifty years that had seemed like so little loomed like an unfulfilled fantasy.

And that was the bitter.

I'd take it. A thousand times over, I'd take it. It was only then, as my thoughts twisted and turned around life, death, and fate, that I realized I was no longer burning.

In fact, I was quite cool.

"What the fuck?"

Will stopped bucking and I rolled away from him cautiously to find Bee standing over us, her face a mask of fear.

"Is he alright? Did I get here in time?"

"Dom!" Sienna pulled up beside her and dropped to her knees. "You're alright. A few burns, but nothing like last time, thank the gods."

Will scrambled to his feet and stared at Bee and then at the sky, uncomprehending.

"How?"

Her lips trembled into a shaky smile and she shrugged. "Tech."

Sienna was already holding her hands over me, sending healing power through my entire body, but even she paused to eye Bethany.

"Remember that massive bag I brought with me? It was filled with something I had asked the wolf tech team to work on. I figured as smart as they are, they probably had done loads of research on the vampire sun shield. Turned out I was right. They'd already reverse engineered it and learned how to disable it in case they ever needed a nuclear option. It only took them a couple days to use that same technology to make mini-sun shields." She grinned as she gestured to a black box a few yards away that looked like nothing more than a wide-barreled utility flashlight.

Amazing.

She continued on in a rush. "Granted, they said they weren't sure they were ready for primetime yet, but I packed a dozen of them just in case we got stuck in

Werewolf Territory while transporting our wounded back or something. Looks like it's working! Elka and the wolves are almost done setting the rest out every twenty yards or so. You just press a button and they're activated, creating an invisible protective barrier that blocks the UV rays."

Will and I both scanned the battle grounds to find vampires in clusters, gathered around the devices as they wept in relief.

The screams had ceased.

"Unreal." Will shook his head in disbelief. "You're a marvel. You brilliant, beautiful creature, you."

He yanked her toward him and kissed her hard on the mouth.

She chuckled and pulled away. "I didn't do it. I'm just the delivery girl."

"And you got here just in time. Just bloody brilliant," Will said, smoothing the hair from her bloodied face before turning to glare down at me. "You, on the other hand. How stupid could you be? I should put you in the dungeon for your insolence."

"You might be king, but I am still your older brother, your general, and your protector," I said, watching the blisters on my hands fade. "Better get used to it."

Will's frown dissolved and he bent to take my forearm and pull me to my feet.

"I love you, brother."

"And I you," I grunted, lifting Sienna to stand beside me. "Which is why we can't just stand out here and risk getting baked alive. We don't know how long the shields will hold. We need to get everyone into the Tower and sort out the good apples from the rotten."

"Agreed."

An hour later, we were safely shielded by the cool stones of the North Tower. The wolves had been key to ensuring that every last vampire alive when Edmund had turned off the sun shield was still alive now. I would forever be indebted to them, because many of the soldiers on the battlefield, I'd trained myself.

And, in spite of their actions, I could not hold on to my anger. Not once I found out the lengths Edmund had gone to in order to ensure their cooperation.

"General, please forgive me. He had a stake to my daughter's heart."

"He lined us up and demanded fealty. Those who defied him lost their heads then and there."

From then until nighttime, stories of his actions went

on and on. In the end, even the majority of those who had been loyal to him of their own accord now denounced him.

"I heard him say it himself. If he couldn't live, then neither would we."

"A monster."

Those did not get a free pass as many of the soldiers had. William stripped many of titles, and others were given prison sentences. A handful—those who displayed Edmund's love of cruelty—paid with their lives.

As with any kingdom, there would be others. Snakes in the grass that might still be among us, but the new monarch had started his reign in the same fashion he intended to continue it. By being fair, and evenhanded, and good.

"We did it," Sienna whispered as she leaned into me, lacing her fingers with mine as we stepped out of the tower and into the night for a moment alone. "Jordan is avenged, Edmund is dead, and we are together."

As she kissed me, I realized what a fickle motherfucker I was.

Because once again, my heart grieved.

Fifty years with this woman would never do...

CHAPTER 25

Sienna

I stared in the mirror, turning this way and that, and then frowned. It wasn't that I didn't like the dress. As far as dresses went, the traditional, blood-red coronation gown was a real looker. Lace from top to bottom, fit to a T, hugging every curve on the way down. It was just...a lot. After so much strife, combat, and misery, it should've felt nice to dress up for an occasion and feel normal and pretty for once. Instead, I couldn't wait to get out of the thing, yank on some pants, and take Havoc for a ride.

Besides, there was still so much to be done...

"I see that look on your face and you need to stop," Dominic called from the doorway. "For the next two days, we're going to take it easy. Enjoy the party, mingle and charm the natives. Once we've solidified our alliance with Diana's people, we can go back home and start figuring out the future and how we're going to restore the Veil. Alright?"

I let out a sigh and chewed my lower lip. "Alright. But I'm having second thoughts about the dress. Are we sure it needs to be this tight?"

"Needs? No. But are you wearing the hell out of it?" He nodded slowly. "You are. Come on now Starshine, or we're going to be late."

Dominic came up behind me and laid a hand on my hip, giving it a squeeze.

"Unless of course you want us to be late..." he raised one brow, the warmth in his gaze growing hotter.

"You need to stop looking at me like that right now!" I shot back, ignoring the fluttering low in my belly as I skittered away with a laugh. "I spent nearly two hours on my hair, and I'm not having you mess it up for a quickie."

"Oh, love..." he drawled, advancing on me. "I never said anything about a quickie. I swear I'll take my time and make it worth your while. You won't even care about your hair by the time we're done."

My brain went temporarily offline as he reached me, and I instantly melted against him.

"Can you two give it a rest?" Raven grumbled from just outside the doorway. "You're making me wish I'd brought a date."

Dominic shot his friend a quelling glare. "You're making me wish I brought a stake. Can't you see I'm in the middle of something here?"

"Not yet, unless you're doing it wrong, which I wouldn't doubt," he replied with a wink. "But in any case, the Queen requires our presence in the courtyard. The ceremony is set to begin."

The ceremony was exactly that. Not a true inauguration—that had already been done the day before at Blackthorne Castle, a week after the battle at the North Tower. This was a ceremonial feast in former enemy territory to celebrate Will's crowning. Basically, an excuse to party and create continued goodwill and camaraderie between the wolves and vampires...and me, whatever the fuck I was.

I shoved aside the subtle, lingering sense of unrest I'd been feeling, and patted Dom on the shoulder.

"Rain check, big guy."

He caught my chin in his hand and crushed his mouth to mine in a searing kiss before pulling away.

"Count on it."

Raven groaned in disgust and the three of us made our way downstairs.

When we reached the great room, the rest of our crew was already present. Will and Bee stood beside the crackling fireplace, chatting softly, as Myrr and Diana sat on one of the sofas with their heads close in deep discussion. Lycan, the Duchess and Lochlin stood in a circle listening intently to something Nicholas of Southwind was saying. It was only then that I realized that everyone I cared about was in this room...in this Realm.

How it had happened, I would never understand. I raised a hand to the butterfly pin in my hair and said a silent prayer for its previous owner. Hannah had been her name, and she'd killed herself with that pin to avoid being purchased at the auction and facing the terrifying unknown.

If she'd been bought by the vampires and joined the Harvest Games, would she have escaped Edmund's wrath and lived?

Only a few of us had.

Could she have been happy here?

I'd never know. All I did know was that those pens and auctions were a thing of the past. At least for the wolves and vampires who would, by decree of both Diana and Will, never again deal in the peddling of humans. When

I asked Will about feeding for the vampires, he said that there were plenty of others who'd offer blood without a pen.

Will had smiled and patted my shoulder. "You need only look to a library or bookstore to find some willing bibliophile enamored with our kind."

Would the rest in the Empire of Magic agree? Only time would tell.

Baby steps. One foot in front of the other equaled progress. We just had to keep pushing for change.

"Ready, then?" Diana asked as she stood and eyed us all questioningly.

"As ever," Will said with a nod.

"Let's show the people a good time, then," the Queen said with a rare smile. "I think everyone deserves it."

We headed to the courtyard as a unit, with three of Diana's personal guards trailing behind her. As we stepped outside, I couldn't help but marvel at the changes. What had acted as our armory and sparring grounds had been transformed into a Victorian-style garden, lush with flowers and greenery despite the nip in the air. Long tables, already groaning with the weight of the food set atop them, circled the perimeter of the massive space and Myrr clapped her hands with delight.

"I, for one, am going to enjoy this greatly."

Hundreds of well-wishers, vampires, and wolves alike, spread across the grounds, talking quietly in circles, still largely of their own kind, but some mixing in.

Baby steps.

"Feel anything?" I asked Dom as we moved closer to the east side of the courtyard, which was exposed to the sun.

"Nope. They've really outdone themselves."

At Diana's request, the wolf tech team had rushed to create two larger sun shields. One to protect the space, and a backup...just in case. Yet another symbol of alliance between the territories that went a long way to easing tensions.

I felt confident that, because of Will and Diana's desire to make it work, this was the beginning of a long and fruitful relationship. One that could be the cornerstone of getting other territories on board to create a unified force with one goal.

To restore the Veil before it was too late.

I thought of Dom's description of the demon rhinos he'd gone a few rounds with at the North Tower and winced.

Some factions would be easier than others, but at least there was hope.

Diana, Will, Evangeline, and Lycan broke away from our little group and moved toward a dais at the front of the courtyard.

Diana stepped forward and held up a hand. With just that regal gesture, the chatter scattered and then ceased.

"We four stand before you, the old guard and the new, to usher in an era unlike one we've ever experienced," she said, gesturing to the others beside her with a solemn nod of respect. "One of peace, and cooperation, and harmony. One of safety, for our families and yours. I could not be more proud to—"

"Traitor!"

The lone voice came from a man just ten yards away, but even Diana's fastest guard couldn't reach him in time as he lifted his bow and fired.

Time seemed to slow then. Dominic lurched toward his sister, even as shouts rang out. I stood frozen in place, watching in horror as Lycan launched himself in front of Diana and took an arrow straight to the heart.

For a moment, the world went silent as a tinny buzzing sounded in my ears and chaos reigned. Two of Diana's personal guards dove on top of her, protecting her from further attack with their bodies, as the third led the melee, swarming the shooter. Dominic yanked me into his arms, mouth moving, but I couldn't hear what he was saying.

It was Evangeline's scream that finally broke through the haze of shock.

"Nooo!"

I wriggled away from Dom and rushed to Lycan's side. His breathing was labored and crackling, his craggy face pale.

"Lycan?" I whispered frantically as I dropped to my knees beside him. The stone floor was already sticky with blood, but I ignored it, holding my hands over his wound. "I'm going to fix it. It's alright, you're going to be okay." Evangeline knelt beside me and took his hand.

"The child is magic, my love," she murmured, voice choked with tears. "She can do it, so just hang on for me."

Lycan's pulse was growing weaker and more erratic despite my efforts, and panic settled in my gut. Just like Jordan.

I looked up to Dom. "Should we break off the end of the arrow and try to remove it first?"

But it was Lycan who replied.

"Gold-tipped." He winced and shook his head weakly even as he tightened his fingers around his beloved's. "'Tis too late, Eva. I can feel it coursing through me even now, but it's alright. I always said I'd have traded a lifetime for just one night in your arms. I meant it. I die this day, a happy man."

He stared at the Duchess like she'd hung the sun and the stars and the moon. And then he smiled.

"Take care of our girls, yeah?"

Evangeline shook her head frantically, skirts rustling as she pressed herself closer. "No, please don't say those things, my heart." She looked up at me, her teary eyes pleading. "Sienna!"

I didn't waste the energy on a reply. I was too busy forcing every bit of it into Lycan's deteriorating body, to no avail, just like with Jordan. How could this be happening again? Why wasn't it working?

"Love..."

"Stop talking!" I snapped back at Dom. "I need to focus, damn it!"

But try as I might, I couldn't find even that weak connection now. The old wolf's heart had stopped beating.

"Sienna..." This time, it was Diana talking.

Diana, crown gone and forgotten, face stained with tears, eyes devoid of light as she spoke again.

"It's over. He's gone."

Hours later, we sat in the great room in silence. Me, Dominic, Will, Bee, and Diana. The Duchess was in her chambers saying her final goodbyes to her beloved alone. We'd all changed out of our finery, and the guests had all gone home.

Except the one who had killed Lycan.

Once we'd known for certain the old king was dead, something had happened to Evangeline. She had become someone else. Something else that I'd never seen before.

Gone was the cultured, sophisticated lady with a quiet power I so admired. And what took her place was terrifying. One moment, she was kneeling on the floor beside me, Lycan's hand in her own as she rocked back and forth, a keening wail building in her throat, breaking my heart. The next, she was rising. Slowly. Surely. And when I saw her face again, it was a mask of pain and hatred, so all-encompassing that it shook me to my core.

As I thought on it now, it still seemed unreal, even in this place full of impossibilities. How fast she moved, like a blip on a screen, as she leapt across the stone floor to the people that had pinned down the shooter. They scattered, tossed through the air like bowling pins after a strike as she tore them away until all that remained was a solitary figure.

"I demand a trial," he said, scuttling backward like a crab as she descended on him, slowly now.

"A trial?" Her smile was chilling. "Haven't you heard? It's already concluded, and I hereby sentence you to death. May you suffer for all eternity," she hissed, eyes flashing, fangs gleaming as she tore into him.

I looked away, but not before I saw the gruesome, first strike.

Now, in the aftermath, it all felt like a bad dream. Except Lycan was still gone, and his blood stained the stones of the courtyard.

"We will need to do some major glad-handing here," Diana was saying, her gaze firmly locked on the fireplace in front of her. "This is going to spook a lot of people from both territories." She shot a quick glance over her shoulder at Will, who stood with his arm around a softly weeping Bee's waist. "We should confab later today about how we want to handle this. Maybe a joint statement to start, and then—"

"Stop it," Will murmured, shaking his head slowly. "Just stop. The politics can wait. We all need a minute, you most of all, to process what happened. To mourn Lycan and find our feet again."

She let out a short, mirthless laugh.

"Spoken like a man who's been king for a day. Damage control is priority one. Surely you all realize that?" The room was silent. She scanned the rest of our faces and then shrugged. "Fine. You can all sit here and cry in your soup if you like, but I've got work to do."

She stalked away as if Edmund himself was nipping at her heels, leaving the rest of us to watch her go.

"She doesn't mean it," I said softly once she was gone. "She's still in shock. The grief will come, and when it does, she's going to need us all there to help her through it."

Dom gave my hand a squeeze and nodded. "We'll be here when she's ready."

"Soup actually sounds like a lovely and comforting idea," Bee said with a sniff. "Why don't I go make some for us all, then? I'm sure the Duchess won't eat, but I need to do something..."

"I'll come with you," Will said with a nod of understanding.

The others drifted away shortly after, leaving me and Dom alone. Instantly, I curled into him, letting the warmth of his big body soothe me.

"I thought it was over. Not the whole thing, of course. But the war between wolves and vampires. I thought we'd have a reprieve...some time to heal. Now this..."

"Talking to Lochlin, I think it is over, except for a select few. Our truce truly is a boon for us all. But there are still wolves suffering from madness, and I would venture to guess he was one of them. The doctors will do an autopsy to determine that, but of course there will always be those who want to keep hate alive, mad, or otherwise. We just need to be hyper-diligent going forward. Weapons checks before public gatherings, that sort of thing. I've already approached General Whalen about sharing protocols and training practices to ensure nothing like this will ever happen again."

I pressed my face into his chest, trying to shut out the image of Lycan's body sprawled on that stone floor.

"Evangeline will need us."

Every time I thought of it, I felt like I was going to vomit.

To have waited all those years to be with her true love, only to have him ripped away.

"And she will have us," Dom said, his voice ringing with resolve.

"Sorry to intrude, but I need a moment alone with Sienna, if I could."

I pulled away from Dom to see Myrr hobbling toward us, her brow even more wrinkled than usual.

"I'll go peek in on the Duchess, then see if I can find something to eat. See you shortly," Dom said, bending to kiss my forehead before heading upstairs.

He was barely out of the room when Myrr wheeled back to face me. "I fear Lycan's death may have broken something inside your Duchess," she said, wringing her gnarled hands together. "The things she's saying don't make sense. She keeps asking me for a prophecy, but as you know, it doesn't work like that. She thinks—"

She stopped mid-sentence and her eyes went wide even as her body stiffened.

"Corumbra..." That male voice again. "You have taken vital steps towards saving the empires and the world, but you mustn't stop here. You need to be protected at all costs. Surround yourself with those that love you, for without you, there is no them. No anything at all."

"Please, don't go yet. I need help!" I begged, rushing toward Myrr and taking her hand as I tried to calm the wild pounding of my heart. "No more of this cryptic nonsense. I don't know what to do next!"

"Stay close to home. Stay alive until your siblings within the shadows are found. Only then can you restore the Veil."

"How am I supposed to find them if I stay close to home?" I demanded, so full of confusion and sadness, I could barely think straight.

"That is not your journey, Corumbra. That is a task for another."

"So, I'm supposed to just sit here and cry in my soup while I wait?" I demanded, co-opting Diana's phrase, anger rising in me.

"If you wish to see a future where the seas are brimming with life again. Where the forest thrives, flowers bloom, and eggs hatch...Maybe even eggs of your own, Corumbra."

I stared at her, uncomprehending for a second. "What did you just say?"

"A child, Corumbra. Maybe even two in your future."

I hadn't even dared to hope it. And still hope bloomed only to be dashed.

"Only to leave my mate and our offspring to watch me wither and die?"

Even as I said the words, I hated myself. I had no right to complain. No right to wish for more. Not when I had a chance at so much more than Evangeline had ever gotten.

"Alas, Corumbra, you and the other keys inherited more than just the weight of the Veil on your shoulders. You were also each blessed with two gifts. The first is singular to each key. The second was given to all of you; Everlasting life. So long as you keep safe from those who would harm you, you shall never die."

Everlasting life.

I was immortal?

I should've asked more questions. Pressed for more details...but by the time I found my voice again, Myrr was once again milky-eyed and frowning.

"That damned deity just took over my body again, didn't he?" she demanded, rubbing at her forehead. "That is unnerving, to say the least. Give me an old-fashioned prophecy any day." She studied my face and frowned. "You look like I've hit you upside with a brick. Are you alright?"

"Yes. I'm just...overwhelmed, is all."

"There was some venison stew already made," Dominic said as he stepped back in the room with a steaming crock. "If you are done with her, Myrr?" he asked, brows raised.

"I'm done," she confirmed with a nod. "Was there more of that stew in the kitchen, by chance?"

"Eat mine," I said, grateful I didn't have to. My stomach was in knots and eating was the last thing on my mind. I turned to a frowning Dom. "Let's take Havoc for a ride and get some air. I'll have some of Bee's soup when we get back."

He seemed like he wanted to fight me on it but stopped himself, instead, handing the stew over to Myrr without argument.

Without looking back to ensure he followed, I rushed out to the stables, restless legs churning as I ran.

"Are you about to do something crazy?" Dom asked as he jogged next to me. "I won't try to stop you, I've learned my lesson, but it *would* be helpful if I could get a warning."

"Nope. You're safe with me...for now." We reached the stables to find Timmy there watering the horses. "How's my girl?" I asked as we approached.

"Pretty amazing, miss. Shall I saddle her up for you?"

I shook my head. "Not necessary. We're going to take her bareback instead."

Dominic let out a snort. "Care to share what's *not* crazy about that, Starshine?"

"Me and my girl have an arrangement, so she's going to be on her best behavior from here on out. Even with you."

A few minutes later, we were both astride Havoc, and I had Dom's arms wrapped around my waist. I gave her a squeeze with my thighs, and we were off and running.

And then we were flying. Havoc's brand new, glossy feathered wings had unfurled and sent us soaring upward, into the night sky. The female Hunter and I had somehow, together, managed to heal her and give her the gift of flight. I still couldn't quite believe it.

"I don't think I'll ever get used to this," Dominic admitted, his grip on my waist tightening. "Fighting off an army of demons? Fine by me. Flying through the sky on horseback without a parachute, never mind a saddle? I seriously think something must be wrong with me to even let you do this."

"Well then, you'll be thrilled to know about the news I just got..."

I told Dominic about the other keys. About everlasting

life, and our children. And, even in the face of grief, we rejoiced. There would still be trials along the way. Things would get worse before they got better, but if we succeeded? The rewards would be so rich. Friends, family, peace, and best of all? My mate.

I would never take it for granted. Not a single day of it. I would fight hard and love harder. Because no matter how cruel it could be, this world was worth saving—Havoc did a loop in the sky and Dom's fingers tightened around my waist as he pulled me closer—but at least I didn't have to save it alone.

Epilogue

Diana

One month later...

I buried my face in Lycan's worn, cable-knit sweater as I lowered myself to the bed, a sob breaking from my chest.

It still smelled like him...leather and spice.

I knew it would take time before it stopped hurting this bad, but until then I'd have settled for just a day's respite. *One* day when it didn't feel like my chest had been cleaved in two.

"Oh, Father...how am I supposed to lead our people when all I can think of is how much I miss you?"

The first few days, I'd managed. It was a blur of activity as I planned his services and dealt with diplomacy issues and tried not to have a complete and total breakdown that might shake the confidence of my people. But when the keep went dark and quiet?

I came completely unglued. Like tonight.

Why hadn't I seen it coming? Why hadn't I made sure that attendees were unarmed, just as a precautionary measure?

Because you're a good leader, and you trust your people as they trust you, a little voice in my head supplied helpfully.

That voice sounded a lot like Lycan's..."And look what that cost me?" I whispered with a ragged laugh.

But time stopped for no man. Not even one as great as my father. The king of wolves with no obligation to me at all, except that he'd made a promise to his beloved to care for me. And what he'd given had gone so far and above that. He could've passed me off to another clan. Watched me grow up from afar and ensured that I was safe. Instead, he took me into his home. Made me a part of his family in every sense. Taught me how to rule with a firm but fair hand. Taught me how to love and be loved.

And now he was gone.

He had died, to save me.

"Get on with it, Diana," I muttered, moving to toss the sweater aside but yanking it over my head instead. "This room isn't going to empty itself."

It had taken a while to work up to, but I probably could've put it off another few weeks. It was just that, all the reminders here were a constant lure and if I wasn't careful, I could end up going mad in this bedroom. Looking through his things, staring at old photos, and pawing through vinyl records he'd played for me as a child...

A gust of wind outside howled as big chunks of hail clattered against the windowpanes.

Time was ticking out there. The weather had continued to decline, growing more erratic by day. If we didn't find the other keys, and soon, we were going to reach a point of no return. I'd already lost Lycan, and the Duchess, gods protect her, was a mere ghost of herself. She'd stayed behind when the others had gone home. She said it was just until she knew I would be okay, but I feared it was more than that. She barely ate, barely spoke, and spent more time in the library with books than she did with people. It was almost as if I'd lost both of them.

And I wasn't willing to sacrifice more than that.

With a renewed sense of purpose, I padded toward his desk, trailing my fingers over the smooth surface. For the next three hours, I cleaned. Taking down pictures in frames, packing some in boxes, setting others aside for myself or Evangeline. Folding clothes and emptying drawers. It was only when I reached the albums that I stopped short.

Maybe just once more, for old time's sake...

For a werewolf who loved our own culture's music, Lycan also had a deep love of music from the human realm. Especially the 1950's doowop style. His favorite?

The Duke of Earl.

It was only recently that I realized the lyrics must have been the kicker.

I tugged it from its cover and slipped the vinyl disc onto the record player. Then, I turned it on and set the needle.

The second the music started, tears poured from my eyes, and I cried in a way I hadn't yet. In deep, racking sobs that came from my soul and made my chest hurt.

"And when I hold you, you'll be my Duchess. Duchess of Earl."

"Damn it, Dad," I muttered, swiping the tears and snot from my face, and reaching for the cover again.

Time to turn off the music and send the servants up to finish this awful job.

But when I moved to return the record to its home, a slip

of paper fluttered to the floor.

I bent low, heart pounding, as I picked up the paper in one, shaky hand. My father's looping cursive covered the sheet, and I swallowed hard and began to read...

If you've found this, Diana, that means I am gone. Likely too old and too slow to keep up with the pups in battle. Such is life. What you need to know most of all is that you were my greatest joy. I cannot imagine how empty my life would've been without you in it, and if that was all my Evangeline ever gave to me, it would've been enough. I am so proud of you, and all you've accomplished. You are already a better leader than I ever was.

Enough of that, though. Now, for the hard bit.

I hate to burden you further, my daughter, but I'm afraid it can't be helped. I've been in search of something that might help us fix what has been broken. Something The Oracle told me in secret could save you all. Years ago, when I was still king and you were more trusting, a man came to our keep. Charming, silver-tongued, and handsome. That man left our territory with a jewel he had no right to take. We need to get it back, daughter. Only then can we find the other keys...

Only then can we restore the Veil.

I stared down at the words, blurring before my eyes as a

memory stole over me. I remembered that silver-tongued snake well. He'd left with more than just the ruby gemstone. He'd also taken a piece of my heart.

I crumpled the paper in my hand, a sense of steely determination coursing through me, softening the grief in its shadow.

I had a purpose now. And my purpose was to find Maverick Wilder, that spineless, thieving bastard, and get back what he'd taken from me.

All of it...and then some.

Scan the code above to pre-order CAGED BY FATE.

Scan the code below to sign up for a release day reminder.

Made in United States
Troutdale, OR
06/15/2023